A Selection of Short, Sometimes Very Short, Stories

N L Hancox

First published as a collection in 2024.
ISBN 9798320346472
All rights reserved.

This book is for
Margaret, Mark and Duncan

Contents

Introduction
10

The Beginning

Once Upon a Time
13

A Personal Element And About The Malvern Area

Water, Water
15

Cracks
18

Sunday Lunch
21

The Duel
24

Summer Weather
27

Purpose?
38

Maybe An Element Of Me

Career Change
39

Bombs Away
47

Uncle Charlie is Coming
49

Peel Back
57

Things Ain't What They Used To Be
64

Sometimes With A Touch Of Fantasy/Surrealism

What If…
70

A Suitable Gent
72

The Future
75

Festive Frolics
77

The Silver Spoon
80

A Clean Shave
84

Koala Control
85

A Horticultural Dialogue
88

Deadline Monday
90

Where Did He Go?
94

Through a Glass Darkly
97

A Murder Mystery
100

Let's Build A Snowman
103

The Sorcerer's Apprentice
107

Janet and John
110

Feeding Charlie
116

The Public Library – A Romance In One Volume
123

What Did I Say?
130

The House of Dreams
136

Margarine
141

Vaguely Biblical?

Clothes Doth A (Wo)man Make
146

There's An Awful Lot Of It In Brazil
148

Dialogue and Word Play

What Is Life For?
155

Assorted Brief (If Inaccurate) Reviews
157

A Conversation For Two
160

Opera Café
162

CCP Not PPE
164

Who's Coming To Dinner?
166

Art Stories

Dinner For Two
169

O & E
174

The Painted Lady
176

Pigment
183

The Kiss
188

History Or Something!

A Letter To My Agent
192

William S And Fame
194

Adieu, Goodbye, Farewell
197

The Path
199

The Path Revisited
202

Based On Nursery Rhymes/Myths

Another Cautionary Tale
207

JJWUTH
210

A Tribute

I Remember
213

My Inspiration
215

An Item of Memory
217

Are We There Yet?
219

Finale

The Last Hill
224

A Selection of Short, Sometimes Very Short, Stories

Introduction

In the Beginning was the Word.

Story telling has, surely, always been part of human culture.

My writing includes flash fiction, 300 – 500 words; some longer stories, rarely much more than 2000 words; and vignettes, brief, funny, sad, off-beat, sardonic, pieces. I like playing with reality, introducing inanimate objects and animals, surreal situations. I write for my own satisfaction or amusement, to try to say something I regard as interesting or important, or simply to entertain. I like to play with words and, if I think it is appropriate, grammar as well.

I have divided the contents into sections. The stories in each section may bear some vague connection or not!

Apart from friends and myself (both disguised), and imaginary characters, I often refer to others from fairy stories, nursery rhymes or to political figures from the last thirty or so years. You may or may not recognise some of these folk.

Different authors have different styles and readers will respond to these in various ways. My own writing tends to be quite terse, and I mostly enjoy reading similar work.

Several tutors, including Ann Schlee, Clare Morgan and especially Sara Banerji, and many fellow writers and students have helped me in my writing, but the final result is what I want irrespective of advice, criticism, or what is regarded as correct.

Introduction

My special thanks to my wife, Margaret, who has encouraged me to publish my stories, and inserted all the commas and hyphens that I forgot to include.

Neil Hancox
February 2024

The Beginning

The Beginning

Once Upon a Time

All good stories start with two people in a supermarket.

'How about a trip to Waitrose?' Adam said, as he reviewed the contents of the fridge.

'Just let me fix my hair,' she replied. 'You get the list, any special offer tokens and don't forget your cards.'

The happy couple picked up a trolley and a self-scanner and set to work cruising the aisles.

'We've broccoli, leeks, radishes and onions,' Adam said. 'We need one more for our five a day.'

'Apples!' his wife exclaimed. 'Look, Granny Smith, Jazz, no, I think I'll have a pack of Painted Lady.'

That evening, sitting on their veranda, Eve took a delicate bite from the firm flesh. The juice dribbled down her chin and her wonky back tooth held.

Slowly the realisation spread through her body. She reached for her phone to tweet her nakedness to the world.

Adam wasn't fazed. He thought she had a great body, but he didn't want everyone gazing at his missus, so he nipped down to the bottom of the garden and grabbed a few fig leaves.

'Try these,' he said, 'to cover the – um – naughty bits.'

And that's what they did, until they could go to Primark for some genuine Bangladeshi cotton.

Happy? Of course, eight billion descendants and growing.

Mother Earth sighed. If only Eve had reached for a banana, things would have been so very different.

13 August 2017

A Personal Element and About the Malvern Area

A Personal Element and About the Malvern Area

Water, Water

Peter was bored. The family was spending a day or so in the country with his grandparents. The adults were doing adult things. He had no school friends here; he had read his book and the batteries in the radio were flat.

As he mooched around the garden at the side of the house, wondering if he should risk granddad Ben's wrath by picking an apple, he heard the front gate squeak. An old man, who looked much like his granddad, came in pushing a bicycle. It was the eyes that were different. One was normal, the other like a blob of white, bloodshot, jelly. The boy forced himself to look away.

'Mornin', Ben,' the man called out.

Ben appeared. 'Here's your stuff, Bill. You be early.'

'Got a job down at Fletcher's farm. Lookin' for more water.'

Peter couldn't help it. 'Are you a water diviner?' he asked.

His granddad glared at him. Bill laughed. 'Let the boy be, Ben. He wants to know.'

He turned to Peter. 'That's right, young 'un. I be a dowser. Same thing, really. Do you want to see how it's done?'

'Yes, please.'

The three of them, joined by Peter's father, walked into the adjoining paddock. Bill extracted a forked piece of wood – hazel, he explained – from a pocket. The Y-shaped object was about 6 inches long, the wood as thick as a man's thumb and the stem of the Y sharpened to a point.

Bill grasped the rod by the shorter arms and walked across the grass with the pointed stem in front. Suddenly the forked hazel twisted violently. The pointed end moved up and down and Peter knew why one of Bill's eyes was so strange – he must have been divining when the rod shot up and hit his face.

'Water down there,' Bill announced.

Peter wanted to dig down, but the adults had lost interest and disappeared for a cup of tea. What was it with grown-ups?

After lunch, Peter badgered his dad to help him find a hazel branch. Armed with an old saw and a knife they invaded the nearby wood.

'That looks about right.' The boy pointed to a forked branch. Dad did the rest.

'Let's try it out in the paddock,' Peter said. They both took turns, walking back and forth. Nothing.

Ben appeared, looked at the rod and shook his head. 'That ain't no hazel, its ash or summat. Course it won't work.'

16 September 2023

Note

Some years later, at university, Peter met an American student, Bill H, who said that a pair of L shaped wire rods, with the shorter end in a loosely fitting plastic tube, were standard issue in plumbing stores in the USA, used for detecting buried gas pipes. The shorter ends were held in either hand and when over a pipe the longer lengths crossed. That evening, a group of them tried out the idea with a pair of bent metal coat hangers. The rods moved when Bill used them, but Peter still drew a blank. They could hardly dig up the quad.

A Selection of Short, Sometimes Very Short, Stories

Cracks

'There's a crack in the ceiling,' his wife said, pointing to the far corner of the kitchen.

He thought it better to agree rather than point out that it was the plaster rather than the ceiling that was cracked. That distinction could wait for later in the day.

While she battled with the crossword he let his mind wander, back many decades to the late 1940s. He was in his grandmother's front parlour, the best room that was never used, as the visitors who came to see her and his granddad were more at home in the kitchen. It was an austere, cold room. A fireplace which had never hosted a fire, a tiled floor covered with a few rag rugs, and an uncomfortable suite finished in a finger-pricking pseudo velvet which penetrated under his fingernails. All of this was watched over by a black and white picture, three elegantly dressed young ladies who were looking with apprehension and excitement at two cavaliers duelling, frozen in time for three hundred years. He had asked his mother what was happening.

'The men are fighting,' she said, 'to decide who asks the girls if they would like to go to the ball with him.'

It made no sense to an eight-year-old, but his attention was diverted as his grandmother hobbled in supported by her walking stick, followed by Mr Bird, painter, decorator, carpenter and general handyman.

His grandmother pointed to the ceiling. 'It's all cracked,' she said, leaning on her daughter while she pointed with her stick at the offending damage.

Mr Bird removed his cap, scratched at his thinning white hair and peered at the ceiling through pale watery eyes. He chewed on the stem of his unlit pipe, considered the situation and agreed. The boundary between every piece of plaster board was indeed cracked.

'Well?'

'Best thing I can do,' he said, 'is to get some wooded laths, nail them over the cracks and then cover it all with a coat of paint.'

'We can't leave it like this,' grandmother said, 'so go ahead.'

The boy remembered visiting a few weeks later. The floor of the front parlour and the suite were covered in white sheets, while three young ladies still watched in anticipation to see which swordsman would thrust first. The cracks in the ceiling had disappeared underneath thin strips of wood. In the centre of the room was a step ladder and a small bench. Mr Bird, in blue overalls, prized open a tin of Walpamur to reveal an 'off-white' colour paint.

He looked at the boy. 'Good stuff this,' he said. 'Don't stain your hands like oil paint and it dries quick.'

He levered out a large lump of congealed paint into a tray. 'You have to add some water to it and mix it up a bit,' he said, 'then you brushes it on. Better get out the way, lad, or your mother will complain if you comes out off-white.'

'There, finished it,' his wife said, pushing the crossword over to her husband and jolting him back to 2023.

'Well done.' He paused. 'I think we'll get a plasterer and decorator into repair and repaint the ceiling.'

She nodded. 'I'll make some calls now.'

He would have liked to have done the job himself, but he didn't think his wife would appreciate wooden strips on the ceiling and he had none of the painting skills of long-gone Mr Bird.

As he finished his tea he wondered if two cavaliers were still being watched by three expectant young ladies. Possibly somewhere but not in his grandmother's front parlour. That and the ceiling had long gone.

He shivered. Time moves forward and carries us with it. One day we would all go the way of the front parlour.

15 April 2023

Note

Walpamur was a colour wash paint. Nowadays you would use a vinyl silk or matt emulsion paint.

A Personal Element and About the Malvern Area

Sunday Lunch

'Peter, help your granddad take Sunday lunch down to Azar.'

The ten-year-old looked at his mother's worried face. He was hungry himself, but he knew he must help out.

'OK, Mum.'

His granny put meat, potatoes and cabbage on a large enamel plate, added some gravy, covered it all with another plate and wrapped both in a thick tea cloth. On another dish she put a hunk of steamed apple pie and custard. Granddad took the first course and, with Peter clutching the pudding to his chest, they set off down the hill.

'Watch out for cars, lad,' granddad said and then walked on in silence. Five minutes later they arrived at the gate to Azar's field.

'Shut the gate, lad, and be careful because the grass is uneven.'

Peter kept a tight hold on his offering.

The brown caravan was in a corner of the field close to the road. A plume of smoke wound up from a thin black chimney. Inside Peter could see a stove, a table and a couple of chairs and an old man.

'Mornin', Azar,' his granddad called out.

'Mornin', Ben,' the old man replied, and added, 'Hello, lad.'

Azar James, of indeterminate age, clambered down the steps at the front of his caravan. The boy saw two dark eyes peering out under the peak of a dirty cap and a dark face partly covered with greying stubble. The shirt was collarless like his granddad's, with the sleeves rolled up to show battered brown arms. He wore a greasy grey waistcoat, matching trousers and black boots.

'Stop staring, lad, it's rude.'

'Oh leave him be, Ben, I don't expect he's ever seen a real gypsy close to.'

Peter blushed and gave Azar the dish he was carrying.

'Thank 'ee lad, that'll go down real well.' He put both plates on the steps of the caravan and started to eat.

'Thank Eliza,' he called out to Ben and then, turning to Peter, he said, 'You come back down here 'bout three o'clock and I'll show you summat.'

Peter was restless after his own lunch.

'Don't you want to read or play?' his mother asked.

He shook his head. 'I want to go back to see Azar.'

'Off you go,' his granny said, 'and mind the cars on the road.'

Azar was sitting on the caravan steps, puffing away at an old pipe. He got up when he saw Peter coming towards him. 'Hello lad, they've let you out, I see. Come along with I.'

They started walking. 'Never mind the old horse,' Azar said when he saw Peter move quickly away from the animal, 'He won't hurt you. He's so old he ain't even curious anymore.'

At the far corner of the field, Azar pointed to the spot where the two hedges met. 'If you look down at the bottom there, you can see the gap.'

Peter stared hard and thought he saw the edge of an old ditch. He didn't like to disappoint Azar so he nodded. 'Yes, I see it.' It was a white lie he told himself but excusable.

'That,' Azar continued, 'is where this world and the next 'un meet. One day we shall all go through there. We don't get no choice.' He puffed on his pipe and began to walk back to the caravan.

Peter thanked him for showing him the gap and went back to his grandparents carrying the plates and dishes.

A week had gone by.

'Are we taking Azar's dinner down?' he asked on Sunday.

His granddad shook his head. 'No need to, now. He was found dead in his chair a couple of days ago. Won't be needin' anything your grandmother can give him no more.'

Peter wandered out into the orchard after lunch. He plucked at some dead grass heads and kicked at a thistle. So Azar had died but he'd really gone through the gap between the two worlds. One day I'll follow him, the boy thought, but not for a long time.

He tossed a stone at an old crow sitting in the branches of an apple tree. Did the bird grin at him or was it his imagination? Peter couldn't make up his mind.

29 October 2012

A Selection of Short, Sometimes Very Short, Stories

The Duel

The boy picked up the axe. He felt the weight of the hard grey steel head and ran his fingers over the smooth, curved ash wood handle. Would the ground metal cutting edge really be sharp enough to shave the stubble off his chin?

'Are you ready, Peter?' a voice called out.

His father sounded reluctant, even sad.

'Coming, Dad,' the boy shouted back, forgetting about his chin and collecting a length of tattered blue nylon rope and a bow saw.

He swung the axe nonchalantly over his shoulder and joined his father, who was carrying a home-made wooden ladder. The two of them walked through the orchard. The dew covered their boots and wetted the bottoms of their trousers. They had to lift the rusty metal gate off its hinges to get into the field that sloped gently up towards a quiet, rutted, lane. Along this boundary ran a wiry hedge and a dozen or so cider apple and pear trees, twisted and battered by winter gales and old age.

His father pointed to a tree almost at the end of the row. It leant away from the slope of the ground and overhung the narrow lane. If it blew down, it would block it completely.

'That's the one,' he said to his son in a quiet voice. After a moment he added reassuringly, 'Should be a good morning's work.'

They fixed the rope around the top of the trunk so that the tree would fall into the field when they pulled.

A Personal Element and About the Malvern Area

Peter, brimming with enthusiasm, was about to start swinging the axe, when his father shook his head.

'Hang on a minute, we've got to cut into the trunk facing the lane first.'

This was awkward work. Half in the ditch and half in the hawthorn hedge. There was no room to use the axe or push the bow saw properly. Peter soon tired and left the job to his Dad. Despite the age gap of nearly fifty years the father had, in the boy's eyes, almost unbelievable strength and stamina.

They rested for five minutes. His father nodded to him, and Peter started to initiate the axe properly. He thought that an axe sang through the air, bit deep into the timber and sprayed wood chips everywhere. His first blow nearly ended in disaster as the metal blade glanced across the bark and the handle twisted violently in the boy's hands. The second attempt was, maybe, better. The axe head wedged itself firmly in the wood and it took all Peter's strength to remove it. In a few minutes his hands were beginning to blister but in compensation there was a growing yellow gap at the base of the tree. The boy was done for the moment and handed over to his father. Then the two of them then took turns to work the axe and hold the rope taut.

Suddenly his father yelled out, 'Keep hold of the rope, she's going,' and then ran back to help the boy. They rocked the tree back and forwards a few times. The splintering wood gave a faint groan. There was a swishing sound as the tree crashed towards them. Some branches splintered on impact but there was enough resilience in the falling wooden lattice for it to bounce up defiantly from the earth before finally subsiding in a static tangle.

Peter was jubilant. 'We've done it, Dad,' he shouted at the top of his voice. Then added, 'I'm going to start lopping off the branches.' He grabbed the axe and ran. His father sighed. He wanted his son to remember that this tree had once been young, living, fruitful, that it was eighty years old now. There was no point, though, in explaining his thoughts to the boy. It would go over his head. Such is the way of the world.

27 February 2001 and 8 July 2002

A Personal Element and About the Malvern Area

Summer Weather

Peter stood on the bottom bar of the green picket gate, gazing down the country road. Heat seemed to lie over the fields in thick, solid, layers. The boy's fingers picked automatically at the curling flakes of green paint on the woodwork.

'Peter.'

He jumped guiltily at the sound of his grandmother's voice.

'Take this down to your Aunt Clara please,' the voice continued, as the old lady appeared round the corner of the house.

He looked at the letter his grandmother was holding.

'It's too hot to go all that way,' he began in a sulky tone.

'Rubbish, boy, it's no but a mile or so. Any nine-year-old can do that. If you start now you'll be back in time for supper.'

He knew it was no good arguing. He took the letter, pushed it into his trouser pocket, opened the gate and set out. It'll serve them right if I die of thirst by the wayside, he thought. This helped him for the first half mile. All the way down to the little stream and through the orchard. His mother had told him a few days ago that it was all right to walk there because it was a public right of way. But he mustn't touch any of the apples. Who'd want to? he thought. They were all horrible, sour, cookers and today there were wasps everywhere. An added peril.

A Selection of Short, Sometimes Very Short, Stories

He'd cheered up by the time he was past the church and on to the common land, today without sheep, cars or visitors. He had a new idea. There was no one in sight. He could experiment – with spitting. This was a disgusting habit, everybody said. It didn't stop his granddad, though. Peter's first attempt was a miserable failure. The spit dribbled down his chin and onto his shirt front. He walked on a few yards, sat down on a hummock of grass and worked the saliva round and round in his mouth. He balled up the liquid, pushed his head back and propelled the saliva forward with a flick of the head and tongue. The results were immensely satisfying. The globule landed on a nearby tuft of grass and set it vibrating. There wasn't as much body in it, he noted, as when his granddad did it. That would come with practice and anyway he didn't cough like granddad.

The triumph soon wore off and he was aware of being very hot and uncomfortable. His shirt was sticking to his back and his trousers felt greasy. The long grass was making his legs itch. Then he remembered the vicar had been talking about spitting, too, in church last Sunday. Some bit in the Bible where Jesus cured a blind man by spitting in the dust and putting the mixture on the man's eyes. That really did sound disgusting. None of the grown-ups seemed to mind, though. His mother had remarked that it was an excellent sermon. It was no good asking the adults for an explanation. They took no notice or told you not to be cheeky.

He could see his aunt's square, dull-looking, brick house, now. The hedge at the front was a straggly mess and the gate was painted a flaky white, rather than green. Apart from that it reminded him of his

A Personal Element and About the Malvern Area

grandparents' house. He ignored the front door. Anybody using that in the country was a total stranger. The back door was open. His aunt was sitting at the scrubbed kitchen table. Behind her a jumble of cupboards, and to one side a sink with a hand pump and a coal fired range. He knew that the sink did not drain properly because he had been told off last time he was here for pouring water into it. The range had to be alight to boil the kettle. However hot the day felt, grown-ups needed a constant supply of boiling water to make the tea that kept them going. That was another fact he knew about the country.

'Hello, Auntie,' he greeted the old lady.

'What do you want, boy?' she answered in a surprisingly strong and deep voice for someone who looked so old.

How old was she? Peter had heard talk of people living for eighty and ninety years. She must be one of those. Her hair was much darker and thicker than his granny's. And the face was just as brown, but so wrinkled that he could hardly tell where her eyes and mouth began, and the skin finished. And how did she survive in that thick black dress which seemed to cover her from neck to ankle? The hands, the only other part of her body he could see, were mostly bone outlined with blue veins.

'Well, boy, what do you want?' she said a second time.

He stopped looking at her, pulled the letter from his pocket and handed it to the old lady.

'One of them,' she remarked as she pushed it aside.

'I expect you're thirsty. Would you like some lemonade?' she added, pointing to the side of the sink.

A Selection of Short, Sometimes Very Short, Stories

Peter collected the bottle and a nearby glass. He hoped it was clean. He sat down at the table and struggled for a moment with the metal spring holding the china stopper with its rubber washer firmly in place against the top of the bottle. Then the warm, sticky liquid gushed into the glass, down his throat and all over his chin and shirt front. Peter coughed. It reminded him of his first attempt at spitting. Aunt Clara smiled.

He noticed that she had stopped calling him boy and seemed less scary. He suddenly felt bolder.

'Is it true, Auntie, that you can make it rain?' he asked.

She looked at him suspiciously and then nodded slowly. 'Could be, sometimes.'

'Would you try now?' he asked excitedly.

Clara got to her feet, slipped a bottle into the folds of her dress, and told Peter to collect several bunches of dried grasses and herbs which were hanging on the wall above the table.

'And a box of matches,' she added as an afterthought.

He followed her into the back garden and laid the bunches of dried material on a bare patch of soil. Clara sat down in an old rocking chair, supervising.

'Now get some branches from over by the fence,' she ordered. After several forays, Peter had built up quite a substantial bonfire. The old lady inspected it, threw some powder on it, had Peter pull her chair a little further away and then commanded, 'Light it and be careful. I don't want you going up as well.'

The boy took a match and, standing as far back as he could, flicked it across the rough strip on the side of the box. The match flared. He thrust it into the tinder and ran back towards his aunt. The flames waited a moment and then accelerated through the dry material. The blaze was spectacular but brief.

'Now we just have to be patient,' the old lady said, 'and you'd best be getting back.'

Peter thanked Aunt Clara for the lemonade, hoped it would rain soon and started the return journey.

He was feeling in a good mood as he approached his grandmother's house. Supper would be bread and fat bacon. It always was. He would cut the fat away and his granddad would tell him it was the best part. Some things never changed. At least he had managed to avoid scalded milk and have lemonade to drink. A quick wash in the sink, a trip 'out the back' and it was off to a long, dreamless, sleep.

The new day was decidedly cooler. After breakfast Peter went out into the field behind his grandmother's house to play around the old pigsty. His grandmother's black cat left its place in the kitchen and came with him. The storm suddenly rolled over the hills and enveloped them in huge, stinging chunks of warm water. As he tore back to the kitchen, Peter momentarily wondered whether God was spitting at him. Cat and boy made it through the door at the same moment, narrowly missing the postman.

'Careful,' his granddad yelled.

'Sorry,' Peter muttered as he tried to disappear into a corner.

The postman continued to address the adults. 'There were your Clara,' he said, 'at eight o'clock this morning in the back garden in 'er old rocking chair. Thought 'er 'ad 'ad it.'

Peter gulped and shuddered. She must be dead, and he'd killed her with that silly rain spell. He would have to own up at once. Grown-ups always found out the truth. Before he could speak the postman added his punch line.

'Sly old girl 'ad been drinking. Made 'er a cup a tea and she were as right as rain.'

Peter let out his breath and wondered what they would have for lunch. He was hungry again.

8 August 2000

A Personal Element and About the Malvern Area

Purpose?

The brambles curled out from the hedgerow, over the ditch and partly covered the broken track. Their ripe black fruit glinted in the strong sunlight. I knew that JJ would not be interested or diverted. He continued his progress down the lane, searching out each step, looking for stability. The warm sunlight recharged his batteries, sending power through his veins.

I couldn't say his progress was either purposeful or purposeless, since I don't believe that he had a concept of purpose. Neither is it true to refer to him, or to change the form of address to her. 'It' would be more appropriate, though I have become used to the male pronoun over time.

The small lane was familiar to both of us. It ran eastwards towards the main road, along the edge of a gentle ridge. Its surface was made of broken bricks and lumps of granite pounded into the ground and then worn and eroded by wheels, feet and rain. The few houses bordering it were shells now. At the far end, deep among the fields, where JJ had started his ramble, the red corrugated sheets that made 'The San' were rotting. The weather, small animals and plants were attacking the interior.

Further down the lane was a house named Rest Harrow, half hidden by tall nondescript trees fighting against the ivy. I had always been frightened when I was a child going to its front door, by the cloying wooded darkness of these trees. Inside had been kindly and welcoming, neat, frozen in an era well before my remembrance. In spring and summer, the garden was swathes of colour blending into the rank grass of the adjacent field and then leading the eye down to the small village half a mile to the south. The two old ladies who used to live there would not have been upset by its present state; they understood that everything returns to the earth.

I followed JJ discreetly, plucking at the ripe berries which made a pleasant dessert to my earlier breakfast. At the mouth of the lane, where it joined the now silent main highway, were two cottages. The first, red brick, with a skewed garage, still clutched at its small orchard. The roof of the carpenter's workshop had collapsed, and the once shiny, sharp tools were rusting. The well cover was still in place. That was good. Who wanted to tumble eighty feet into the earth to meet a stagnant pool of water?

The larger dwelling had once been painted from head to toe in cream weatherproof paint, which emphasised its red rimmed metal window frames. The paint had peeled away and the later additions to the house were deteriorating. The fine garage and shed still stood defiant, despite their vacant, staring, doorways. The carefully planted fruit trees forced their way upwards through a thick mass of grass and weeds. I would never play amongst them again, nor risk my grandfather's wrath by picking the plums and apples before they were ripe.

JJ had almost stopped as he approached the main road. Not quite, though. He pushed at the tall grass bank opposite, found it unyielding and turned towards the village. He walked by the small wood and over the stream, guided perhaps by the church spire.

A Personal Element and About the Malvern Area

It would have been useless for me to ask him where he was going, whether he would return home; that is, if he had a home. He would have replied with one of his randomly selected phrases, almost certainly irrelevant, and would then have continued on his way. His brain contained much clever circuitry but lacked direction. One day he would stumble or grow cold and lose his power. Then his rusting bones would join the other debris of our world.

I followed him past the dishevelled church yard and on to the village shop. It surprised me to see a sign advertising tea over its entrance. An open door revealed several tables neatly laid with crockery, knives, forks and serviettes. The smell of cinnamon drifted from the kitchen.

The 'Hello' was bright and cheerful, and came from a young woman with golden hair and deep-set grey eyes. A little girl clutched at her skirt and occasionally peeped around at me.

'Would you like tea?' the woman asked. 'I do white bread and real butter, home made plum jam and cinnamon scones, and you can have a tomato if you wish.' She indicated the bowl of red fruit on the windowsill.

'And proper tea to drink,' the small child added bravely, before she disappeared.

I was hungry by now. 'That sounds good,' I replied.

I ate and drank greedily, though I left a scone for the little girl.

As I paid my bill the young woman touched my arm.

'I know that you grieve for JJ, 'she said in a very formal way. 'You believe that he has no purpose and that you have failed him.'

A Selection of Short, Sometimes Very Short, Stories

I nodded. What else could I do? I was dumbstruck. How could this woman know about my private worries? It was impossible.

'Of course, JJ has purpose,' she said, 'only it's rather limited. He doesn't feel his surroundings. He can't branch out. He has no free will. He is an automaton programmed in a narrow way at birth, or do I mean construction?' She became less serious and smiled at me.

I looked at her skin. It was beginning to age and her dress was less fashionable. I took a deep breath and shook my head to try to clear my thoughts.

'What do you know about free will and automatons?' I challenged.

My words didn't seem to trouble her at all.

'Free will, from the church,' she replied, 'although they were not altogether certain. When I was a young girl,' she continued, 'I had a doll, a rather marvellous doll. When you wound it up, it could walk and talk and turn its head. That was its purpose, but it didn't have an independent mind. Even a country girl like me knew that.'

'Your JJ is a little like my doll. One day he will run out of power and pass away,' she said, 'but you still have the gift of life and the ability to create again, something better.'

She paused, gave me a virtuous kiss on the cheek and squeezed my hand. Her dress lengthened and turned to black as she melted before me.

I looked around the dusty, soundless, room, bemused. Through half focused eyes I noticed an old postcard propped up on a shelf. It was a British seaside scene, from, maybe, a century ago. I examined the faded sepia picture and turned it over. I could just decipher Lina where the address had been written. I remembered the name then. She had been old, and I was so young and like all youth I knew everything and had never listened to her stories.

I checked my watch. I still had a long way to go. I returned to the road and began to search for JJ. The way forward was across the wide common land, a new territory for both of us. There would be no brambles there. I had better take the scone I had set aside for the young child to sustain me.

27 October 2009

Maybe an Element of Me

Career Change

Lizzie pushed open the study door. Her husband was in his characteristic pose, hunched over the keyboard, peering at the monitor screen and surrounded by untidy layers of books and papers.

'Remember, darling we've visitors coming for lunch,' she said, 'and you promised to light the barbecue. In time for us to eat before the middle of the afternoon,' she added for emphasis.

She regretted the annoyance that had crept into her voice. If only Roger would think less about the economy of Roman Britain and more about everyday life in the twenty first century. Today was a special occasion.

'What are you writing about?' she asked by way of a peace offering.

'The effects of coinage, as distinct from barter, on trade,' he replied in the pedantic way he used when speaking about his work.

He recognised his wife's edginess and decided to omit the details of the place and period referred to in his article.

'Sorry, the barbecue quite slipped my mind. I've just reached a natural break though, so I'll start ignition right away.'

It was a balmy June day. The charcoal was soon glowing, and Roger settled in a comfortable reclining chair with a glass of red wine. Life was good. Work that interested him, a loving wife, and even his teenage son and daughter were more bearable than he had been led to believe. I wonder who our visitors are? Lizzie had been evasive when he'd inquired. Today, he was relaxed; he didn't care.

'Could I disturb your reverie for a moment?' Lizzie smiled at him. 'We do need more chairs and a few small tables. And how about some more,' she hesitated, 'smarter trousers and a clean shirt?'

He noticed that his wife had ditched casual jeans for a summer dress. It must be an important occasion.

'OK, will do.' He finished with a mock salute.

'Why,' Lizzie wondered, 'do men never see the obvious?' Her mother had warned her. Not specifically about Roger, but about men in general. Mustn't become acid, though, particularly today. A gulp of Roger's wine restored equilibrium and she returned to preparing the food.

'Watch yer, you old devil. Still conning the students, I hear.' Roger jerked his head round so quickly that he nearly upset his wine. It was Charlie, less his dog collar, clad in a dark jacket and black pin stripe trousers, his head shaven. He was rounder and more rubicund, but Roger supposed that at forty-five you were allowed that, even in the church.

'I thought that you would be in purple gaiters or some such, now that you have been promoted.'

Charlie grinned at Roger's idea of modern church dress.

'Then you might have felt that you should address me as "My Lord Bishop".' So, I thought I would come in mufti.'

The ringing tone came from inside Charlie's jacket. He pulled out his mobile and laughed. 'Never know, it might be the Almighty needing a bit of advice.'

'Shut up, Charlie, and switch the damn thing off.'

The bishop pretended to be a little offended, nodded to his wife, Martha, and the phone was silenced. 'Do I get a kiss?' Martha asked Roger.

'Just a kiss,' Charlie said, 'not a ten-minute clinch.'

Martha was delectable and Roger strove to recall the appropriate one of the Ten Commandments. Or was it two? Today her figure was enhanced by a long, shimmering dress. She managed to combine sex and sweetness in equal parts, no doubt helped by the rumoured monthly allowance from her father, who could never understand the mutual chemistry between the lovers. Father, being an Episcopalian, would presumably be disapproving as well as puzzled now, Roger surmised.

Lizzie joined them. 'Peter will soon be here. I had a call from him a minute ago.' While they sat and chatted, the steaks and sausages were set to sizzle on the grill, ready to join the row of accompanying dishes set out on the trestle table.

'Hello.'

There was Peter, no different from two decades ago. Tall, rather ascetic Peter. Destined to be a banker from birth. He had not disappointed. He flicked his jacket off, removed a tie and picked up a glass of wine in one continuous movement.

'Where,' Roger whispered to Lizzie, 'is …?'

'Shh,' she responded, 'he's in between.'

'What are you driving these days?' Roger quickly asked.

'Series V BMW, goes like a dream.'

Roger knew that from Peter this was not a boast. It was a simple statement of fact.

'Food's ready,' Lizzie announced. 'Help yourselves.'

A Selection of Short, Sometimes Very Short, Stories

Casual conversation continued through mouthfuls of meat, salad, bread and wine. Two teenagers appeared like Viking raiders, were polite enough to say 'hello', and then vanished housewards bearing the spoils of their raid, to continue with their own culture.

As a final touch, strawberries and more were washed down with Chablis.

'A toast,' Lizzie proclaimed, 'before we all fall asleep.' Glasses were raised. 'To us.'

Roger looked at his wife and three friends. 'What's that for?' He tossed out the question to anyone who might supply an answer.

No one spoke. They all waited for Lizzie.

'It's our reunion,' she said. 'It was twenty-five years ago today, give or take a day or two, that we all went out as a group for the first time.' She put her arm round Roger's shoulder. 'The five of us had crammed into your dad's old car and went to see a Roman villa in the Cotswolds.'

Gradually the scene came back to Roger. Jumbled at first, but the pieces soon fitted together, and the few memories became an avalanche. Five students, all in their twenties, no cares, not a lot of money. But the day was fine, and they just took off. Charlie brought his girlfriend, Lizzie. She met Roger for the first time. The villa was a random choice. What a setting, though. Gouged out of the escarpment, facing south onto a swathe of small green fields, with the tall trees crowding in at the back. Roger recalled arguing with Charlie as to how the end came. A sneak attack by the barbarians, through the trees, or did their cavalry charge in from the south? Peter had put paid to such romantic nonsense.

'What were his words?'

'The invaders didn't have horses. It was a gradual decline,' he had assured them. 'Eventually the owners found that the estate was not paying, they sold up and moved away to the safety of one of the city settlements.'

Bankers for you!

'Our first problem was that formidable woman on admissions. She said we weren't students. Just because we had forgotten our Students' Union cards. Martha, you did a good job there with your library identification,' Charlie recalled.

'And I had to stop you pinching the offerings out of the sacred fountain, 'Lizzie reminded Peter.

He looked at them rather sheepishly. 'I was preoccupied with an economics essay I had to submit to my tutor a couple of days later,' he explained.

'And you fell into an excavation trench and were told off,' they all chimed at Roger.

'That's permitted to future professors,' he replied somewhat haughtily.

Roger smiled to himself. It had all seemed so spontaneous and simple then. Now, with the hindsight of maturity, he could see that it was anything but. Peter was concerned with his grades. Charlie had been suddenly smitten with Martha and Roger himself was getting over losing his first love and doubting more and more the wisdom of spending another year studying engineering. How was he going to break the news to his father? It was the energy and optimism of youth that helped push the problems aside and let them all enjoy themselves. He could do with a bit more of that now. He guessed that they all could.

'We'd had enough of culture and history after two or three hours,' Roger said. 'It was a beautiful day, time on our hands. We decided to walk up the hillside at the back of the villa, through the trees. Do you all remember?'

'Just to see what there was,' Peter said. 'I think I was looking for a forked hazel branch as an aid to water divining and Charlie and the girls were way ahead enjoying a private joke. You were bringing up the rear, Roger, in a pensive mood, I recall.'

'Roger finally caught up with the rest of us,' Martha said, 'when we made it to the flat area above the trees. 'It was so different from the southern outlook. There was a wide vista of huge chalky fields, divided up with broken down stone walls. The land was green with wheat. Where the track broke out of the trees there were massive chunks of concrete, reinforcing bars and decaying corrugated iron sheeting.'

'There had been an airfield up there in the war,' Peter added.

Lizzie looked across to her husband. 'What do you remember?' she asked him.

'One special thing. I still have that Roman coin I found in the spoil from that rabbit burrow,' he said. 'You know that's what swung it for me. I'd been considering changing my course. The coin did it. Archaeology for me.'

The other four were suddenly silent. The fun and gaiety, the mutual reminiscing, had vanished. Roger shivered. It was unnatural. He looked round them all. Charlie had folded his jacket to make himself a pillow, placed it on a convenient stone in the rockery and was busy flicking ants away, while trying to drink some wine without spilling any down his shirt front. Lizzie was half sitting, half kneeling on the lawn, looking across to the house, in an abstract way as though it might disappear at any moment. Martha, always elegant, reclined on a white plastic chair, steadfastly refusing to meet Roger's eyes. Peter, propped up against the side of the shed with his legs straight out in front of him, was studying his feet intently.

Roger looked from one to another. He was puzzled, again.

They all spoke at once and then all stopped. Lizzie glanced pleadingly at Charlie. 'Your province, I think.'

He sat up, lodged his plate, now devoid of strawberries, between two stones, ignored the ants.

'We made a pact, never to tell you,' he began. 'We suspected that you wanted to change your course away from engineering. It was no accident you finding that Roman coin. It was only meant as a joke. We didn't think you would fall for it. On the way out from the main site we all went into the shop and, while you lot were admiring homemade pots of jam and tea towels, I paid one pound for a Roman denarius.'

'A lot of money for a penurious student,' Peter chipped in.

Martha glared at him and mouthed a most unladylike expression.

Charlie continued. 'You were preoccupied and as we walked up the track. I suggested hiding the coin at the top and getting you to discover it. We thought it would cheer you up. None of us had thought it through, it was simply a silly student prank.'

'What if I hadn't taken a swipe at that pile of earth?' Roger said.

'We had a contingency plan,' Lizzie replied. 'We couldn't waste an expensive prop.' She sounded more confident now. 'If you didn't play, Martha and I were to head you off, while Peter and Charlie put the treasure where you couldn't miss it.'

The group was animated and chattering again. Roger was jolted by the story and his emotions were racing. Be a pro, a small, insistent, voice hammered away in his head. You are always demolishing myths. Now yours has gone. It all happened so long ago. Fate, with a little help from my friends. Predestination? He wasn't in the mood for philosophical conundrums. He'd met his future wife that day, as well as changing his career.

'Fine lot of friends you turned out to be,' he laughed. 'You really hoodwinked me, but I suppose the intentions were harmless. And it hasn't worked out too badly.' He took a long, deep draught of wine, put his arm round Lizzie, kissed her, and relaxed in the sun.

'You would have been a hopeless engineer, anyway,' Peter added. 'It was the girls who got the car going again when we broke down on the way back home.'

30 May 2022

Bombs Away

It was the ultimate 'des-res'. The ideal site. Secluded, quiet, exclusive and it was all mine. OK, Roger and Mickey shared it, sometimes.

The word on the street, although we lived on a road, was that it was the result of a 500lb German bomb. Of course, the Germans, being that continental lot, would use kilogrammes. Probably jettisoned by a damaged aircraft on the way back from a raid on, say, Liverpool. If it wasn't jettisoned then the bomb aimer needed his eyes tested, because it landed on waste ground half a mile from any houses. The blast blew out some windows and killed an old bloke. Poor fellow probably had a heart attack when the siren woke him up and he fell downstairs in the blackout.

That's the potted history. The crater was about ten or twelve feet across, eight feet deep, with a pool of stagnant water in the middle. The soil was reasonably compact. Things weren't so hot in winter as the drainage was a bit suspect, but then I didn't go out to that area in winter. Mother said it was too muddy, I'd ruin my shoes, make a mess of the carpet and, lastly, get pneumonia.

In the spring and summer, the crater was eminently habitable. Rog and I dug some crude steps in one side, fished without success in the puddle of water and constructed a built-in wooden seat on the opposite edge. We could crouch down, have a smoke, except we had no cigarettes, and put the world to rights. Our strategic views were mainly concerned with various teachers at school, why we had to learn Latin and which local girl could we persuade to go to the pictures with us. Since money was short and the girls aloof, we dropped all that and concentrated on making a go cart.

We found an old packing-case-cum-pallet and Mickey scrounged four wheels and two axles from, well we didn't ask. I borrowed Dad's saw, which was very blunt, found some nails and a hammer and a length of rope, and Formula One here we come. Mind you, at the time we had never heard of Formula One but that's what we would have said in retrospect.

There was a handy concrete track not far from the crater and we raced down that. Raced is probably the wrong word as excessive friction and a dodgy front axle made progress slow and erratic.

We had great plans for the coming season. An improved version built by British engineers with vision and determination. I must have seen that rubbish on a newsreel at the local cinema. Disaster. A stout fence was put up around our site. An unexploded bomb? Nothing that exciting. They, the dark forces, started to build houses on our sacred land. Horrible places. How I wished another German bomber would come along with a 1000lb bomb this time. No such luck. More maths, more English, French – ugh, Still couldn't persuade a girl to go to the cinema. It's tough being a kid.

15 September 2021

Uncle Charlie is Coming

My mother broke the news on a Saturday morning at breakfast. Uncle Charlie would be coming to stay with us 'for a short while.'

Who was he, and for how long? were my silent questions as I continued to chase the remains of a fried egg around my plate and use it to capture the residue of baked beans.

She looked at me and smiled her slightly enigmatic smile, though I still don't associate her with the Mona Lisa. 'That means,' she continued, 'that you will have to leave your bedroom and move to the attic room. It's not really an attic,' she continued, 'just a little smaller …'

'… and with that broom cupboard at one end,' I interrupted. A ten-year-old's rebellion surfaced in the eternal question, 'Why?'

'Uncle Charlie,' she explained rather hesitantly, 'was my father's much older brother and has nowhere else to go.' I wanted more details, why had I never heard of him before, questions, questions all to no effect. Discussion closed.

We were a nuclear family, mother, father, son. My mother was in her forties; my father, although claiming eternal youth was a decade or so older. There was one set of very aged grandparents whom we rarely saw, the other set had simply disappeared; an occurrence I took in my stride with youthful indifference. Remote relatives, or were they friends, appeared occasionally, patted my head and possibly provided sweets or a book. Their origins were apparently from pre-war days when mother had worked as a secretary, or was it book-keeper, in and around the Birmingham area. I tried to make sense of it all and then gave up and listened to the radio, usually programmes that my mother thought were 'not quite nice'. I had an ally there, in my father, though even so I never made it past 8.30 p.m. before it was off to bed.

I sulked, moved a few of my treasures and waited. A week later, on another Saturday morning, a taxi arrived with Uncle Charlie plus a leather suitcase that was big, battered and brown. Dad worked in the motor car industry and there was another crisis at the factory, a breakdown on the production line I expect, so mother welcomed the old man to our house. 'You take the suitcase,' she said to me, 'up to the back bedroom.'

Uncle Charlie's luggage was heavy and the handle on the case badly worn. I struggled up the stairs and dropped my load on the floor of the bedroom, my old room, pushing the case into a corner with my foot.

'Come on down and meet your uncle,' Mother shouted up, in a tone that indicated to my well attuned antennae that she was stressed. I caught my breath and ran downstairs.

The memories I have of Uncle, fifty or sixty years later, are of polished boots, which were soon replaced by carpet slippers with scuffed toes, brown corduroy trousers supported by braces and a belt, a waistcoat, a shirt with no collar, not much hair, steel rimmed glasses and a pipe. As I recall, this garb hardly varied for Uncle Charlie's whole stay. Another thing I remember was the pocket watch, secured by a chain to a buttonhole in the waistcoat. 'That'll outlast me, lad,' were the first words he said to me, and were periodically repeated. I suppose it did outlast him, though I don't know where it went, but pocket watches are not fashionable anymore so it's probably not important. My mother was strict about the pipe. It could be emptied, refilled and smoked outside but inside my uncle was only allowed to suck or chew the stem. Nevertheless, this seemed to give him some satisfaction.

There was a tour of the house and garden. Uncle Charlie's walking stick pointed out plenty of weeds and there were a few comments on the vegetables Dad and I attempted to grow; well, Dad did the growing and I did the attempting.

Our house, on the northern edge of Birmingham, was a compact 1930s build, at the top of a short steep drive. There were old folks to the left and old folks to the right. Though the neighbours were pleasant enough the important thing was not to make too much noise, something that hampered football on the back lawn with Dad or school friends. I pointed out once to my mother that the woman on one side of our house played the piano very loudly and with not a hint of a harmony or rhythm. That, however, I was told, was of no consequence. Apparently, there were differing standards of noise toleration, or the quality of the noise, depending on age. I didn't push it, instead I practised whistling out of tune whenever I saw the old dear. To be fair I usually whistled out of tune anyway, as alas I had not inherited my mother's musical ear.

We were neither rich nor poor, but careful with our spending, though my 6d a week pocket money was easily frittered away. Sometimes I was embarrassed by my shiny new shoes or smart jacket compared with the clothes of other children round and about. Dad, as

I have mentioned, was in the motor car industry, a job he disliked, while mother looked after the home front.

I thought that an advantage of Uncle Charlie's stay might be a change in what we ate. The war and post-war menu was basic and filling, not always appetising. Perhaps the dreaded India rubber tripe would be replaced by an eatable dish; would chips with vinegar and salt be permitted? Alas the former stayed on our plates and the latter was, my mother said, 'very bad for you as it dissolved the lining of your stomach.' I never knew if this statement was true or not, since this delicacy never appeared, whether wrapped in newspaper or on china plate. At least we had suet dumplings for a treat now and then.

Many decades later, I occasionally have chips, with vinegar and salt, and no ill effects so far, and how I wish you could get some real suet dumplings. I expect that nowadays those are one of the things that are bad for you. I reckon its all fashion.

Uncle Charlie started the day with breakfast and a large cup of sweet milky tea, and then spent half an hour shaving with a cut-throat razor sharpened on a leather strop. Afterwards he would sit, half read the newspaper and mutter a lot. His paper was the *News Chronicle* with the *News of the World* on a Sunday. That seemed a more engaging publication to me, but it was soon replaced with the upmarket, and less salacious, *Sunday Express*. In that paper the most interesting articles were inside exposures of Russian espionage and British traitors, which seemed to be as prevalent as the amorous activities of the other large section of the British public.

On most days Uncle Charlie took a turn around the garden. I was often seconded as accompaniment in case

Maybe an Element of Me

he tripped, collapsed, or was otherwise in difficulties. Fortunately, my services were never required. He was wary of unripe fruit or vegetables and would moan, 'You'll get the belly ache if you eat that,' when I took a firm tasty apple from one of our trees. Left to the natural ripening process this variety of fruit was soft and unpleasant to taste and feel in the mouth. He warned me and I ignored him.

Once a year we, the family, went off to the seaside and had the pleasures of a week or fortnight in a boarding house, in my experience run by a plump and formidable woman. There were outside attractions such as crowded cinemas where my mother was sure 'you would catch all types of known and unknown and lethal germs,' sand, seaweed, flotsam and jetsam – I once found a battered tin of fruit that had come from a wrecked ship. This was still a period of post-war austerity and you had to be in the right place at the right time to get an ice cream. The downside was that you had to be out of your lodgings, sun or rain, by 10.00 a.m. and were not allowed back until 5.00 p.m. I recall several long wet walks, with my father singing and recalling his army days in an attempt to 'keep our spirits up.' Uncle Charlie was not up to these rigours, and neither could he be left on his own, so for one or was it two years this type of rest and relaxation was 'out of the question.'

I began to get used to Uncle, meaning, if I am honest, that I ignored him, with a dash of resentment. My football career progressed; I became reserve for the school's third team. With the help of my father, I built several small hot air balloons. For those of you who wish to try this, you need a cylindrical wire framework about three feet high, covered with tissue paper but leaving the bottom open. Across this bottom opening you attach a small metal dish filled with cotton wool soaked in methylated spirit. When ignited, the hot gases produced fill the balloon, which floats off into the sky. When the fuel is exhausted the balloon falls to the ground. In retrospect, doing this in a built-up area was very irresponsible. It is odd that, as otherwise law-abiding citizens, this never occurred to either of us.

It was Uncle Charlie's shortness of breath that first alerted me to something being 'not quite right.' The old boy could barely make it up the stairs. The solution was to bring the bed downstairs to the back room, removing the sofa and pushing the upright piano into one corner. This put my career as a pianist on hold and probably saved the sanity of the unfortunate woman who tried to teach me. My hands were all right, but I had two left ears, that's the polite version.

Uncle Charlie's health did not improve, and my mother spent more and more time 'nursing' him. Dad and I could fend for ourselves, but I was unhappy with my mother always seeming tired and tetchy. Then one day when I returned from school, I was told that, 'Uncle Charlie had been taken to hospital that morning and had since died.' I was shocked but I don't think I felt any loss. Now we would have two rooms downstairs and I would get my mother back.

Shortly after the funeral my mother gave me an envelope. 'This is from your uncle,' she said. I ignored the fact that I did not regard him as a true uncle, whatever I had been told, and opened the envelope. Inside were five old-fashioned £5 notes, wafer thin as though they had been printed on tissue paper. 'It was his life savings,' she said, 'and he wanted you to have them because you were kind to him.' I had not expected this, or any, gift. I thought of myself as a breezy schoolboy, not bothered about 'old folk', and I began to regret the many times I had ignored my uncle or been impatient with his stories, eager to get away. It was my turn to mumble something I hoped was appropriate. I spent some of the money and a few weeks later bought National Savings certificates with the remainder.

Many decades later, retired from the legal profession, my football career having stalled aged around eleven, I was sorting through some old documents, at my wife's behest. As she put it, without adornment, 'Remember the Boy Scouts motto,' and then, 'You don't want our children to have to go through endless filing cabinets full of your stuff do you, so why not cut down on time when you are in the clubhouse after a round of losing balls on the golf course and sort your papers out yourself.' Dear me, one foot in the grave already.

Most of the material was eminently shreddable. I was an optimist but there appeared to be nothing among my papers that an American university, anxious to build up its archives, would wish to purchase. The most interesting find was three handwritten sheets of paper. It was my mother's writing; I recognised her characteristic 'r'. Each was headed, 'Dictated by Uncle Charlie.' There was no date. I read through the script once, twice. There were no great revelations. He had had a succession of very ordinary jobs, mainly working on farms; he had loved once and lost; he had very little money, and that was it.

'You are very quiet,' my wife said at dinner that night, 'not like you.'

I explained what I had found earlier among my papers. 'That took me back to when I was ten or so,' I explained, 'and to Uncle Charlie. I was not very pleasant to him and resented the time my mother spent with him in his final days. He deserved better than that,' I concluded.

Several months of research on the internet enabled me to locate the old man's final resting place. His body had been cremated and his ashes were in the cemetery close to where I had grown up.

'What are we doing here?' my wife enquired, one bright summer day, 'and you in a suit,' she added.

'To pay my last respects,' I said, 'to an ordinary old man who left me his life savings even though I ignored him and at times disliked him.'

The council did a good job keeping things neat and tidy. We found the plaque where it should be. I pulled away a few tufts of grass, polished the metal, stood and I said a final, silent, farewell.

It's not pleasant growing old and, after I had managed to put it off for a very long time, that inevitable fate was catching up with me. Time to make my peace.

13 April 2021

Peel Back

'Are you planning a trip?' Charlotte asked her husband across the breakfast table.

'How did you guess?' Edward countered.

'Easily; you are agitated and trying to read the instructions for your SatNav upside down.'

'You win,' he smiled. 'I thought we would go to Birmingham today.'

'But you always say that you don't like driving in towns and cities.'

'This is different. I want to see if I can go back in time.'

Charlotte sighed. He was in one of his fey moods but a trip to Birmingham could be interesting. She loved Oxford but on a grey, tourist riddled day a change was welcome.

'Whereabouts?'

'Hall Green,' Edward replied.

'Isn't that where your cousin Michael grew up?'

Edward nodded.

'I remember you saying you were very close when you were teenagers,' Charlotte said.

'That's right. Then after university he married, went to live in the US and we drifted apart.'

'I remember you were upset when you heard he had died a few months ago,' Charlotte added, 'but you keep these things bottled up, you won't talk about them.'

It was a factual statement. Edward had always guarded his emotions and she had learnt to live with it.

'It's a nostalgic trip, is it?' she continued, trying to lighten the mood, 'to see how the place has changed.'

Edward made no comment.

Charlotte fastened her seat belt and then rummaged through her handbag checking for phone, make-up and glasses. They would probably get lost at some stage of the journey, even with modern technology, and she would be asked to 'look at the map and see exactly where we are', so she needed to be prepared.

Conversation was desultory at first and then died altogether when Edward turned on the radio. 'There might be some travel news,' he explained.

Once the motorway had disgorged them onto the southern outskirts of the city they navigated left turns and right turns, roundabouts and traffic lights for, Charlotte checked her watch again, thirty-five minutes; it seemed like hours. She nearly asked if they were 'there yet' but that phrase didn't seem to mesh with the atmosphere in the car and she kept her counsel.

Eventually, amongst a myriad of streets and roads, Edward suddenly shouted, 'That's it, Tixall Road.'

The explosion of her husband's voice in the confines of their small car jolted Charlotte from contemplation.

Hall Green is one of the conurbation's many suburbs. Rows of identical bow windowed semis, joined at the central wall like Siamese twins, faced each other across a road barely navigable because of parked cars. Each house had a short front garden usually rented out to local weeds or used as a parking space. Paint was peeling off the woodwork, and roofs and chimneys were festooned with dishes and aerials delivering instant Nirvana, Charlotte imagined, to the bored occupants within.

She shivered; the interior of the car felt cold despite the heater valiantly trying to operate at full blast. 'Any chance of a coffee and maybe a bite to eat?' she ventured.

'Later.' Edward was in concentration mode. 'First we must find a place to park and then …' His voice trailed off as car pulled out, leaving a space that appeared to bear no restrictions. Edward backed in at the third attempt.'

'This will do,' he said, 'lets walk back up Tixall Road. Michael used to live on the right, at the start of the rise; there was an awkward lamp post on the edge of his parents' drive; I nearly hit it once or twice when I backed out.' He grinned. 'That was fifty years ago, and I am not that much better at driving now.' His wife maintained a diplomatic silence.

There was no point in sitting in the car, Charlotte thought. She didn't really know where this visit would lead but she might as well go along with events. Perhaps they would stand outside the house and take a photograph, and Edward would tell her at length how things were different then.

They walked along for fifty or sixty yards until Edward stopped and let his shoulders sag. 'Just relaxing the body and hence the mind,' he explained.

He pointed to a house which appeared indistinguishable from the others in the road. 'That's the place. Now we shall see if my theory works.'

'What are you talking about?' Charlotte asked. 'Where's your camera? Are you going to take a picture with me pointing to the front door or the bedroom window?' She was becoming alarmed. Her husband's eyes were darting everywhere as though he expected to be ambushed. Did he think he might see the apparition of his dead cousin?

There was a sheen of perspiration on his face, and he was breathing rapidly. She felt for her phone; who should she call?

While she was mentally debating this question, Edward bent down at the edge of the pavement. 'If you grab the kerbstone firmly between the thumb and first two fingers of the right hand, assuming that you are not left-handed of course, and pull gently and steadily you can peel back the surface of everything, the garden, the house, the neighbour's property, all of it.' He put his hand in place and started to pull upwards. The action and the speech appeared to calm him.

Charlotte couldn't decide what to do. Her body awaited a command, but her mind was paralysed. Her husband could act strangely at times, but this was exceptional, a first. She was standing in Bank Holiday weather, cool and cloud covered, in a suburban part of Birmingham, with her husband crouching down at the edge of the pavement and several onlookers, who had appeared from nowhere, doing what onlookers do – staring and at the same time trying to pretend that this strange couple did not exist.

Slowly Edward stood up and stepped aside, all the while pulling gently at an invisible layer. He strained, gave a final tug and exclaimed, 'There, got it.' He wiped his forehead with the left sleeve of his coat, so as not to loosen his grip.

His wife tried to suppress this bizarre episode; perhaps normality would return, and the event would be recalled later as a mild hallucinatory episode. If she viewed things logically, everything was as it was a couple of minutes ago when they arrived at the spot;

well, nearly everything. She felt colder because the indifferent weather was now augmented by drizzle, and she had to zip up her anorak jacket to her chin. Unlike his wife, Edward began to glow.

'Are you sure you are not looking for an alien presence?' Charlotte joked as she began to wonder if she was as mad as her husband. Whatever it was, she knew she must try to enter into this delusion, if only for the practical reason of getting home that day.

Her husband remained detached, his eyes unfocussed.

'Well, is it working?' she asked sharply.

Edward emerged from his reverie. 'Sort of. The front gardens are much tidier and the paintwork on the houses better. What you would expect for the early 1960s?'

The rain had taken a mind to become more serious. Water trickled down the back of Charlotte's neck as she cursed her decision to buy a fashion statement without a hood. She attempted a smile. 'Your description, Edward, sounds like the product of an imagination well past its sell-by date.'

Ignoring her comment, he added, 'It's not completely correct though. There are people standing around that don't fit; they are from now, not from the sixties; one girl has a mobile phone clamped to her ear.'

Her husband's disappointment began to affect her; she felt herself being dragged into his world and she wondered for a second if the girl with the phone was contacting the police. With an effort she managed to stand back from the scene.

'You don't think these things through, Edward. You can peel back layers of the place but not the human element.' For the spur of the moment, she considered that sounded quite convincing.

'Good point, my dear. I hadn't considered that. I'll have to do some more reading and experiments at home. I never realised that you were so interested in my esoteric theories.'

'Am I?' thought his wife; Maybe, I'm also cold, wet and hungry and I need to get him away from this place before he is permanently deranged. She looked at her husband and surreptitiously tried to summarise forty-two years of marriage on the fingers of her right hand; three children, reasonably normal, a mortgage paid off, and a kind man with an interest in military history, test cricket and homeopathy. It could be worse.

'The first thing to do,' she said, more gently now, 'is to regroup.' This, she surmised, would appeal to the military historian in him. 'Then we can reconsider our tactics. That would be best carried out in a pub. I spotted one at the end of this road and down to the right, it's about five or six minutes' walk away. They may even have an imitation log fire.'

As they walked down, arm in arm, Edward observed,' Not one of my better theories; the more I think about it the crazier it is.' He finished with a smile and planted a brief kiss on his wife's cheek.

The pub greeted the pair with a mixture of warmth, wood smoke escaping from a stove and beer as Edward pushed open the door.

'Sorry about the smoke,' the landlord said; 'it's probably the wind direction.'

Charlotte wondered if she should ask her husband to try going forward in time and conjure up a smokeless imitation fire. Instead, she settled for soup, a roll and coffee. Edward tucked into a baguette and a beer, and they began talking about their next holiday.

Maybe an Element of Me

To the casual observer they were an ordinary middle-aged couple but who knew what really happened in their minds?

1 December 2015

A Selection of Short, Sometimes Very Short, Stories

Things Ain't What They Used To Be

I heard the front door open quietly.

M appeared. She dropped her bag. I gave her a big hug. She smiled despite the tiredness in her eyes.

'Do I feel any different, do I look any different? she asked.

'It's not your hair, and have I seen that purple jacket before?'

'It's mauve and of course you have.'

Oops, I had better try again. I pushed her away to arms' length, held her shoulders and looked at her slowly, top to bottom, side to side.

'Fine detective you'd make,' she said. 'Shall I tell you?'

'I suppose so,' I said.

'I went to the one stop bra shop today,' she announced. 'It's like a porno underwear palace. Some of the sexiest bras you could imagine. Black, pink, white, lacy, embroidered, peek-a-boo. Designed to uplift both morale and body.'

'It must be by run by a sex goddess,' I replied.

M shook her head. 'No, A plain, middle aged matron. Mousey, with a hint of a moustache.'

'May I have a look?' I motioned to her blouse.

'Of course,' M said. 'Take your time though. You're forgetting something. It's not simply the bra. I'm a bit deficient in the filling department. Don't worry. They're into boobs as well. From British Standard, which is about your size,' she added, 'You give them the measurements and they'll mould it. And each item is individually wrapped in soft tissue and boxed, with the inspector's initials and details of the appropriate EC standard stencilled on the top.'

'I might have guessed,' I said, 'a Euro breast.'

I moved in closer for a delicate prod.

'OK, which one is artificial?' she asked.

It was a loaded question. I knew damn well which it was. I'd lived with the knowledge for several months. I pretended to be unsure.

'They feel the same,' I began. 'The right one is just a little more elastic – it springs back more readily when I press it. It's really difficult to tell,' I added trying to be reassuring.

'Good.'

'Would a baby know?'

M laughed. 'Silly question. Babies are much more intelligent than you think.'

Later that evening, while M was showering, I went into the bedroom to select a clean shirt for the morning and there was her prosthesis lying on the bed. By chance? I doubt it. I picked it up. Heavy, strangely cold. A small nipple moulded in place.

I heard footsteps behind me. I jumped at the sound of her voice and dropped the prosthesis guiltily.

'It won't bite.' Her tone was flat, maybe disappointed.

I looked at the device again and then at M.

'The colour is a bit off,' I said.

M. shrugged. 'One tone suits everybody'.

She picked it up, pretended to weigh it in her hand and set it down on a chair.

As we lay together trying to get to sleep, my hand strayed over to the flat ribcage. I had seen the scar many times but had yet to acknowledge it properly. The pre-op nurse had shown us lots of pictures. Torsos with skin pulled tight over the bone, with just a little rucking along the divide.

'Six, nine months in and you hardly notice anything,' she assured us.

My sense of touch confirmed the topography. I'd wait a while before giving it a full visual.

Several months on. Time for a holiday before M was back at work. Gatwick was crowded, departure was delayed. We played a game to pass the time before our flight was called.

'What was the figure you read?' I asked M.

'Maybe four percent,' she replied.

'I guess there are a hundred people in this room,' I said. 'Half are women.'

'There's me and someone else then,' M finished my sentence.

'Who's the other one?'

We picked out a bustling, statuesque, forty-something-year-old. She stooped forward to adjust the strap on her shoe. Her blouse fell away from her body, and we could both have disappeared down the cleavage.

'Wrong,' we said together.

M picked up her book and started on chapter two, again.

The hotel was luxurious. An inviting green, grey swimming pool and a well equipped gymnasium.

'What was the running machine like?' I enquired when M reappeared.

'Good, but I kept slapping.'

I frowned. 'What do you mean?'

'You start resonating when you run,' she explained, 'And the artificial side bounces away from your body. Here, feel for yourself.' She placed my left hand on her polymeric other half and set it into a rhythmic pulsating motion.

I could hear the gurgling slap of silicone against body and feel something different.

It's a good test. Not to be recommended, though, unless you know the other person very well.

A light and lazy lunch was approaching.

'There's only one thing left to conquer,' M announced just as I was ready to tuck in and then have my siesta.

'What's that?' I didn't mean to sound grumpy.

'The swimming pool, stupid.'

I knew I was beaten and ten minutes later I was there covered in trunks, towel and sun cream. M. adjusted the straps on her swimming costume, winked at me and slid into the water. I stuck my toe in. Inviting, but I'd settle for a coffee anytime. There was only one other couple foolish enough to brave the cold of the sun this early in the year. They were reclining about twenty feet away. The woman, of advanced years, was encased in a voluminous bathing suit which still allowed her flesh to creep through every crevice of her chair and slop over its edges. Beside her an anaemic old man surveyed the world with disinterest through spectacles perched halfway down his nose.

M's swimming was getting more adventurous. She ducked her head under the water and a wobbling pink mass of moulded polymer appeared, executing a graceful parabola before effecting re-entry. I could see the old man's eyes widen and a broad grin spread across the wrinkled flesh that composed his face.

'Don't be disgusting, Henry,' the ageing chatelaine by his side intoned as she obscured his view with a towel.

I ran along the pool edge to give M a hand out of the water and if necessary, commence search and rescue.

'No need to worry, you can still excite the male.' I thought I sounded most encouraging. Her lips moved marginally.

I didn't catch what she said, as she grabbed a fistful of the iron band of muscle protruding above my trunks and flicked me into the water.

2001, revised 2 February 2017 and 19 October 2018

Sometimes With A Touch Of Fantasy/Surrealism

A Selection of Short, Sometimes Very Short, Stories

What If…

Said the PM, whoever he or she might be.

'What if, everyone was very, very small?' The voice continued. 'That would solve all our problems, energy, housing, overcrowding.'

A dissenting voice from the end of the Cabinet table interrupted. 'What if these citizens were so small that they couldn't hold a pencil, and were thus unable to make their cross on the ballot paper, then where would we be?'

'Probably in opposition,' another voice boomed.

Eventually a consensus emerged, and it was agreed to send the Minister without Portfolio to Binsey, a semi-rural outpost of the City of Oxford, to consult with the Centrifugal Research Laboratory, a spin-off of the University's Department of Innovative Thinking.

'Good afternoon, Minister.' The attractive young lady with shoulder length hair smiled. Her modest dress bore a label announcing that she was Alice. 'I expect you would like a coffee before you meet our MD.'

The brew was refreshing and welcome, the meeting interesting, the proposal sound, not overly costly and, though the Minister did not admit it, incomprehensible.

As he left, Alice handed him a small silver box. 'One of these pills,' she said, shaking the box, 'dissolved in a glass of water will relax you if you feel stressed.'

She smiled again, though this time a disconcerting, vanishing smile.

Briefcase in hand, the Minister without made his way to No.10 to explain to the assembled members of the Cabinet the outcome of his recent trip to the provinces. Concerned by his inability to know what to say, he slipped one of the special 'relaxation' pills Alice had given him into a glass of water and swallowed the mixture.

A giant slab of blackness descended as he walked into the meeting.

'Didn't know we had ants in here,' a voice boomed, (probably the voice that boomed before). 'Anyway, I've squashed the little devils. Won't give us any more trouble.'

Meanwhile, by means of advanced telepathic communication, in a research laboratory in Binsey, a MD breathed a sigh of satisfaction. Now they could continue their work without interference from politicians. Who knew what they might then achieve?

He knocked back a celebratory G&T and found himself towering above the countryside on a par with the gleaming spires. Oh well, back to the drawing board.

19 August 2022

A Selection of Short, Sometimes Very Short, Stories

A Suitable Gent

I hide behind an ordinary name – Fran. If you are in Cornmarket, you might, if you are very observant, see a middle-aged woman, reasonably slim, crows feet spreading out from the corners of the eyes – good sense of humour, seeking gentleman – 55-65 – for fun, lasting relationship, likes dogs, children (other people's), country pubs and theatre visits. Genuine calls only, please. That should do it.

I never thought I would try this but sipping my glass of wine a few nights ago – just the one I promise, before a TV dinner – my personal imp, said, 'Give it a try.'

The phone rings. 'Hello.' Anticipation, the blood rumbles round the arteries dodging the odd deposits of plaque. I listen.

'You are fifteen and unhappy. Take my advice, dear. Most fifteen-year-olds are unhappy sometimes. It's your hormones, love. Ask your mum about hormones. You don't have a mum. I am sorry. Two ugly sisters who make you cook and clean while they check their mobiles and a dad who is out of work and permanently sloshed. Welcome to Britain 2022.'

'Let me guess. A tanned, handsome guy, greased-down hair, never without his shades, says you look great, could get you into modelling and he's invited you to a party on Saturday night. Cowley Road.'

'Grab one of your sister's tops, clean jeans, fix them a nice supper and off you go.'

God, I'm cynical.

Sometimes With A Touch Of Fantasy/Surrealism

'Hello.' More anticipation. I'll need stents at this rate. 'Oh, it's you Prince Charming. You are not a gentleman, and you are not 55-65. You may look it but that's the drugs and drink acting as a disguise for youth. You are having a ball, Cowley Road, Saturday night. Let me guess – I must be psychic. There will be a fifteen-year-old there who you are grooming for a possible position overseas. You gave her my phone number so that I could persuade her to go, and you want me to clinch the deal with the old glass slipper trick. How much? One hundred and some white powder. Phew, she must be some looker. OK you're on.'

I didn't even hesitate. I'll celebrate with another drink to try to wipe away the taste. A girl's gotta live, and when your big end is knocking, and your ignition is dodgy ... It would be good to meet a nice gent, 55, but that's the stuff of dreams.

Cinderella, eh. Nice name. Having a good time? Yes, so why the worried look. Midnight, the big one two. And it all ends.

The kid is glowing. I wonder what they have been feeding her apart from cheap booze. That's what I dislike about this crowd, everything is cheap.

She has wide apart eyes and a heart shaped face. That's like Polly. She would have been twenty-seven this year, but I left her alone while I ...

'Come here Cinders, here's a hundred quid, now run, damn the glass footwear. Get out now.'

'You let her get away, you bitch.'

Ouch, that loosened my teeth. God, what's that sticky stuff coming out of my side?

'Think she'll make a complaint, Sarge? About her boyfriend.'

'Not this time, he's gone too far. What's this in her pocket? Would like to meet… Well, let's hope there's a kindly gent to welcome her on the other side.

'You're not going religious, are you Sarge?'

'No, just nail the swine.'

2022

Sometimes With A Touch of Fantasy/Surrealism

The Future

A funny thing happened to me on my way to the future. I intended to go to the Forum but there were road works on the way and the bus stopped, or terminated as they say, at the Agora, an interesting word that has just been banned by Wordle, though that is totally irrelevant.

As I sat in one of the seats reserved for the elderly or otherwise handicapped, interrogating the screen of my phone in a random and pointless manner, this most attractive, if I am allowed to say so, young woman came and sat next to me. She was wearing elegant red trainers which transmuted into slim fitting jeans, but I will stop there before the Woke police (query, do they have them in Wokingham or are all the citizens there converted?) provoke a false flag operation and carry me off to the Tower – they would have to carry me as I can't walk that far – to join the two Princes entombed forever in the walls of that historic establishment.

She said to me, somewhat reminiscent of the actress and the bishop, 'Your arrival will vanish instantly because the future will be the past by the time you realise that you are there.'

This charming young person must have been cramming those two-and a-bit pounds of neurons, axions and whatever, that resided behind a few millimetres of bone (sorry about the mixed units, I always buy my cheese in ounces) topped by luscious blond hair, with cod Zen philosophy. So, I smiled, always a good idea, and said, 'I've never thought of that.' And added as an afterthought, 'What do you recommend?'

'I'm hungry, you're loaded–' (It must have been the imitation Rolex bought in the bazaar in Old Cairo Town or my natural insouciance.) '–and I know an excellent vegan restaurant where they still manage to complement their quinoa, chickpeas and green salad with a passable Burgundy or Beaujolais.'

Her words hung in the Covid-free air that separated our heads (there was a hell of a draft from the open windows that would blow all germs and, given the chance, half the passengers away). Over to me.

'Why not?' I said.

I rapidly inserted crispy bacon into our joint diet, and I can say that I've found the future and it really is most pleasant.

18 February 2022

Sometimes With A Touch of Fantasy/Surrealism

Festive Frolics

Being an account by an unreliable narrator, of events neither diverse nor politically correct, that occurred one summer's day, related in an attempt to cheer up those of us hidden behind masks and lock down.

Dawn arose, caressing the weathered stones of Castle Drongo, 'and if you don't wind up that bloody clock,' an annoyed voice belonging to the Lord and Master of much that he could survey said to a shrivelled retainer, 'it'll be the last any of us see of the sunlight.'

Trestle tables scattered about the lawns were piled with pies and ham, chicken and cheese, beef and strawberries, summer fruits, artisan bread, beer, and wine and even sherry for the 'non-drinkers' in anticipation of 3.00 p.m. when the village hordes and sundry retainers would descend upon the annual largesse.

Lord Marchmont fired a blunderbuss in no particular direction to announce that proceedings would commence imminently.

Famished mouths attacked the victuals with gusto, feeding hungry stomachs. The Rev Ebenezer Eglington, confused by the size of the crowd, ascended a large stone in the rock garden and declaimed, 'Today I take my text from Habakkuk,' a minor prophet whose status was, he judged, suitable for the assembled peoples, and began a peroration on the evils of fermentation and fornication. His announcement was misheard by young Master Marchmont, temporally afflicted with a degree of deafness due to a day's shooting, as 'Have the cook,' a muscular matron of suppressed desire. Clasped to her bosom, the youth wondered at her biceps, honed she assured him by years of kneading and baking, the results of which kept Drillit and Fillit, specialists in oral misadventures in the nearby town, adequately reimbursed.

Mistress Viola was found lying amidst the petunias, apparently lifeless, her virginal white décolletage stained crimson. Dr Delilah Doolittle, but recently graduated from medical school, proclaimed 'murder'. PC Percival arrived post haste upon a rusty pedal cycle with his note pad open and pencil tip licked, to ascertain the facts. These proved overwhelming and he sought the solace of a telephone with which to summon Hercule Holmes, investigator extraordinaire. Aroused from a postprandial slumber, the detective arrived to view the body. The crimson stain had spread to the grass. He bent down and gingerly sampled the evidence with a fingertip, this being before the discovery of DNA. 'Raspberry ripple,' he pronounced, at which the supine corpse sat up, belched in a genteel way, and remembered what her governess had told her. 'Don't bolt your food, my dear.'

HH smiled and engaged Dr Doolittle in conversation. 'I didn't think,' he opined, 'that they allowed the gentler gender into the arcane secrets of medicine.' The Rev Eglington, having given up conversion for conversation interjected, 'In view of the appendages which the Almighty in his infinite benevolence has bestowed upon Adam, I should hope not.' Euphemia Eglington calmed her husband, who was, she knew, about to become overheated despite having donned his summer alpaca suit. 'You forget, Ebenezer dearest, that the Almighty, in order to correct this unfortunate oversight, caused the fig tree to develop large leaves.' Theologically bested, the vicar subsided, his hand clasped round a large glass of claret and his nether regions supported by a convenient garden seat.

The musicians arrived: a cellist, two violas, four violinists, a portable harpsichord and a piano accordion player. 'Chopin composed,' the harpsichordist proclaimed. 'And you decomposed,' another voice replied. 'Deconstructed,' the conductor of the ensemble corrected. He tapped his baton on a convenient drainpipe to suppress further argument and they began to massacre Mozart. Sundry youths, who were Brahms and Liszt, seized comely wenches and attempted to dance. Bacchanalia slowly dissipated as the sun sank down pleased to see the end of this frenzied day. Lord Marchmont consumed a large whiskey and another, his duty done for the year.

13 January 2021

A Selection of Short, Sometimes Very Short, Stories

The Silver Spoon

George Buckingham Bulstrode, 1838–1894, was born with a silver spoon protruding from his mouth, an anatomical happenstance which would have been extremely painful for his mother and fatal for the infant, had it not been proverbial.

He spent an idyllic childhood on the family estate, hunting, shooting and fishing with George Buckingham Bulstrode senior, interrupted by only occasional and unsuccessful forays into more conventional education.

Eventually, as he was beginning to succumb to the simple rustic charms of a local milk maid, he was packed off to his father's old college at Oxford. Although not a natural scholar the offer of a generous endowment for the fellows' cellar assured his acceptance.

After three years of indifferent application, interspersed with the more practical side of a young man's education in the pleasures of the field and pursuits of the flesh, he left with a very creditable third and the prospects of the army, the church or dissipation. He chose the latter but alas his plans were interrupted by the demise of his father who passed from earthly existence, due to an excess of port and lack of caution on the hunting field.

The twenty-two-year-old son and heir was bequeathed an estate of approaching 3,000 acres, containing several farms, two livings, a large and dilapidated mansion, a mother given to swooning, and the prospect of a seat in the newly reformed Parliament as a good and true representative of the people of South Worcestershire, at least those of any account.

This was surely a pleasing prospect for any young man. To complete his comfort, and not unaware of their own, his mother, aunts and sundry relatives suggested that he propose to Miss Emily Armstrong, a healthy horsewoman, with a fine seat, and no mean fortune if not looks and charm. Her dowry would repair the west wing and ensure the comfort of all, if not the new Mr Bulstrode senior. In the course of time nature, and Mr and Mrs Bulstrode might facilitate an heir to continue the family name and fortune. Her son, his mother confided to her diary, could always seek solace in other unspecified country pleasures and the cut and thrust of Parliamentary debate, the latter without having the discomfort of needing to arrive at any conclusion.

George Buckingham Bulstrode, Bart., as he now preferred to be known, sat at his desk one day in the estate office, brandy and cigars to hand, farm bailiffs waiting at the door, and considered many things: his finances – adequate; his relatives – tiresome; the prospects of Parliament – boring; Miss Armstrong – frightening; a decent day in the saddle – excellent.

It was at this moment, dear reader, that two events occurred which rendered the aforementioned list irrelevant. A small spider repeatedly attempted to climb from the floor to the desk, bringing to mind the experience of a discomforted Scottish king, whose story had been related to the young man in infancy by a puritanical but sweet governess, and wood smoke drifted into the room through an open window. Under the assault of this combination of influences the brain of George Buckingham Bulstrode, Bart., suffered a momentary and minor seizure.

He saw himself marching through the high savannah of the great African interior, hacking his way through trackless jungle, the unannotated areas in the nursery atlas, bestriding Bulstrodia, a country carved from virgin land, coloured pink and dedicated to the glory of his beloved Queen, Victoria. His mind was made up. Nothing would deflect him. The pleas of his mother, the importuning of the electorate, the smile of Miss Armstrong, all had no effect.

He acquired from his tailor what every modern explorer wore, a brace of firearms from his gunsmith, a ton of canned beef, and a goodly supply of sovereigns and, accompanied by two faithful though unhappy retainers, set sail for the unknown continent.

His adventures there were many. Suffice to say that wracked by dysentery and malaria, he arrived one day at a small settlement in Upper Sudan, there to expire and leave his bones to the dark continent, his soul to God and his hopes to his successors.

Miss Armstrong, so recently presented with the prospect of marital bliss, only to have it snatched away, went into a slow decline. Her encroaching years rendered the prospect of a husband unlikely. She no longer found comfort athwart a horse. On the advice of her clergyman confessor, she took solace in the Word and decided that as a dying gesture she should bring its ample benefits to poor benighted people, less fortunate than herself, who inhabited unmapped areas of the globe.

Modestly covered, belted and encased, she travelled widely but found that her message of hope and enlightenment was usually ignored unless matched by a plenteous supply of material goods.

Disheartened and disillusioned, she one day passed through a small settlement in Upper Sudan, where local gossip informed her that an Englishman lay dying. She called in to offer tea and sympathy to the unconscious soul, unaware that under the parchment like skin and sunken flesh resided the body of her erstwhile suitor.

Her gentle touch stayed the fever and when he awoke his eyes beheld an angel. While still weak and confused, he proposed and was accepted. On being slowly nursed back to health he realised his mistake, but his decadent past was behind him. He was a new man, tested and forged in the heat of the desert and steam of the jungle. His word was now his bond.

The pair exchanged their vows in the presence of an itinerant priest and assuaged their love on the lengthy journey home. On arrival his invalid mother was wheeled out to meet her long-lost son returned from foreign parts. She was surprised at this kind mature man and even more surprised when he introduced the former Miss Armstrong and a bawling infant, George Buckingham Bulstrode, junior, clutching a silver spoon, though alas of the plated variety, presented to him by the charmed midwife who had seen him into the world.

The shock was too much for the ageing chatelaine. She swooned one last time and joined her husband, firstly in the local churchyard and then in heaven.

Her son and his wife settled into domestic country harmony, devoting themselves to the well-being of their tenants and children and even the local wildlife.

Then one day a studious young man sought entrance to his father's college in Oxford. The doors opened to embrace him, but that is another story.

18 December 2019

A Selection of Short, Sometimes Very Short, Stories

A Clean Shave

The landlady's daughter drank my shaving water. I was not well pleased, so I shot her.

The police constable shook his head. 'Nasty job, sir,' he said, extracting his iPad from an inner pocket and laboriously recording the details. 'You'll have to accompany me to the station.'

The judge was Mr Justice Jones. He looked smart; well turned out.

'If I had been christened Justice, would I be sitting there?' I whispered to my defence counsel.

'Don't point, and shut up,' he hissed.

The summing up from the judge concluded with, 'Nasty job, but you must consider all the evidence.'

The foreman pronounced, 'guilty.'

The judge nodded.

I stood.

'In view of the exceptional provocation,' the judge said while stroking his chin, 'I sentence you to do two hundred hours of community service. However, you have to swear to buy and use an electric razor from now onwards, though you are,' he added, 'allowed soap and water to wash behind your ears.'

My lady friend remarked recently on kissing my cheek, how refreshingly smooth it was.

27 September 2016

Sometimes With A Touch of Fantasy/Surrealism

Koala Control

Another day. Forty degrees plus. Another forest fire, maybe?

Ken looked at his wife Kerri and their three hungry cubs. Not everyone relishes an unvaried diet of eucalyptus leaves. Ken, Kerri, Katy, Kylie and Kenau did. And he was aware of the diminishing food supply.

'What a pity,' he said to Kerri, 'that you don't like porridge.'

'What's that?'

'Boiled oats and water.'

'It sounds horrible.'

'Brown bears, black bears, grizzly bears and teddy bears all love it, and polar bears would, too, if it didn't freeze before they could spoon it up.'

Kerri sighed. It was her long suffering, earth mother sigh. The one that united all females from amoebas to zebras, though she recalled Ken telling her that amoebas were asexual and therefore did not count.

'Why don't you amble off to the 4X tavern,' she said, 'and sink a few beers? That way you'll be happy and there will be more eucalyptus leaves for us.'

Sheila, the barmaid, was a beaut and very obliging, so Ken quickly agreed, but not too quickly as to arouse suspicion.

Soon he was propped up, paws on the bar, foam around his face, telling the sheep shearer about his predicament.

A wife, three offspring and, for all he knew, another on the way and not enough eucalyptus leaves to keep

A Selection of Short, Sometimes Very Short, Stories

fur and paws together.

The shearer, a gruff but kindly man, wiped the back of his hand across his mouth. 'Bloody hell, mate you've got problems, too much bloody fertility.'

'Keep it clean.'

The man looked up to see the beautiful Sheila frowning at him between the handles of the beer pumps.

'This is a family pub,' she said. 'We get all sorts in here and some are very impressionable.'

She winked at Ken.

The man muttered an apology and took Ken aside. He whispered for fear of causing further offence. 'Ken, get the missus on the pill. That'll will solve your problems.'

He explained the details, outlined an alternative that brought tears to Ken's eyes and then delivered the clincher.

'You don't look like a celibate monk to me, mate.'

Ken nodded, finished his beer and headed for the 24-hour pharmacy.

Back home he presented the pack of pills to Kerri.

'The end of our problems,' he assured her. 'The supply of eucalyptus leaves will grow, and our family won't.'

She smiled. At last, without a perpetual supply of youngsters she could enrol in a feminist bear assertiveness course, maybe go for something more cerebral.

'Great, Ken.' She kissed his cheek.

The knife paused on its path to behead the egg, as the archbishop reread a sentence in his morning newspaper.

'Get the bishop,' he shouted to his secretary. 'I don't care if he's still in bed, get him.'

The rudely awakened bishop told his secretary to contact the parish priest.

The parish priest listened and promised immediate action. If the church lost control of the animal world, he knew, they all knew, humans would be next. 'And then God help us,' he observed to his curate.

'I thought He did,' the latter replied.

'Don't argue, get on your bike and sort it out.'

Ken and Kerri listened impassively, while Katy, Kylie and Kenau gambolled at their feet.

Ken was beginning to feel guilty. Interfering with nature. He started to nod in agreement with the arguments.

Kerri just smiled and smoked a menthol cigarette. She shook her head. 'Now I've the time,' she said, 'thanks to not being overrun with progeny, I'll be able to study empowerment and become mistress of my destiny. We'll probably join the Universal Church, and I might even try for the ministry.'

She looked across at her husband. 'Don't worry Ken, we'll find something for you to do.'

Ken rolled on his back, legs in the air, eyes glazed and howled to himself. He would never go into a bar again.

6 December 2014

A Selection of Short, Sometimes Very Short, Stories

A Horticultural Dialogue

'Where did I come from, mama?' Bertha the baby beet asked.

Before the embarrassed mother could answer her child, the wise men of the vegetable world, the round, rubicund, Reverend Radish, who tended to repeat himself, Thomas Tomato the Trade Union convener, whose words had to be taken with a pinch of salt, Mustapha the Marrow and sundry yogis and swamis from the outer limits of the British allotment, all began to talk.

Cannelloni Bean, of Italian stock, was oblivious to the chatter as he tried to wind his tendrils around Lutecia Lettuce, who was all heart underneath but flighty on the surface.

'One at a time,' bellowed Parson Potato, a heavily built, nay ponderous preacher, who despite spending much of his life beneath the soil, was surprisingly articulate, though slow of speech. He seized the moment to give his own answer. 'No one knows for sure, but it is believed, at least in the countryside, that you begin life as a seed, sealed in silver foil, in a paper packet.'

Bertha interrupted, 'Is there a picture of me on the packet?'

While Parson Potato mopped his earth encrusted brow, Samuel Spinach, the Socrates of the vegetable world, started to speak. Alas, his words boiled down to very little and that indecisive.

Sometimes With A Touch of Fantasy/Surrealism

George and Gloria, the gourds of government could no longer keep silent, though their contributions were contradictory and unclear.

'You need me to interpret all that,' said Leonard the lawyerly lima bean, but no purse was forthcoming, and he relapsed into silence.'

'Get on with it, you lot,' a voice shouted out from amongst the weeds in an overgrown vegetable bed.

Eyes and faces turned, as though following the sun, and fixed on Colin, a scrawny carrot, much affected by the fly, brought on so it was said by promiscuity and interbreeding.

'As I was about to say,' Mustapha said, flourishing a shiny copy of Monty Don's latest work …

He in turn was shouted down by fellow clerics, commentators and masses of brassica and beans. Fortunately, he has a hard skin and took no obvious offence.

Sadly, at this moment of maximum disharmony, a brown, gnarled, hand descended, grasped Bertha, removed her crowning glory and deposited he remains in a basket

'What have we got for tea, Mum?' young Hamish inquired.

'It's your favourite, son, baby beets pickled in vinegar.'

The fork descended and Bertha disappeared in one gulp, her memorial a none too discreet belch.

10 August 2014

A Selection of Short, Sometimes Very Short, Stories

Deadline Monday

He removed his glasses and rubbed his eyes. Another coffee might help. As he squeezed the plastic cup, dark brown liquid spilt onto the desk, just missing the keyboard. A grubby paper handkerchief mopped up the mess. Might as well re-arrange the papers and pens as well, he thought; anything to put off the moment of creation. The mission statement, pinned to the wall in front of him, grinned and taunted him – **Derrida deconstructs, we reconstruct**. It had caused amusement and ridicule from the others in the office, reinforcing their stereotype of university types who thought that a degree made them superior.

The deadline was 5.00 p.m., this Monday; the requirement 500 words, the subject irrelevant provided it was riveting to a potential 35,000 hurried readers. The result of failure was, he guessed, no desk, no coffee, no pay and it would still be Monday, well, maybe Tuesday. The coffee, as available here, would not be missed, but the pay packet would.

To make certain, he pulled back his sleeve and studied his watch. It told him that it was 3.45 p.m. on Monday afternoon. By the time he had tested that fact from all possible angles, it was 3.46 p.m. This electronically driven time piece had cost him an extra £19 because he had demanded the day of the week to be indicated in letters as well as a number showing the date. And this was how his loving investment was being repaid.

Sometimes With A Touch of Fantasy/Surrealism

His brain – residing, so he had once been reliably told by a friendly medic, between his eyes, ears and a receding mop of hair – was desiccated, possibly due to the consumption of half a bottle of vodka the night before. It was not firing creatively, not generating those ideas for which brains are, allegedly, famous.

Maybe if he shut his eyes and let his fingers wander over the keyboard, something would appear. It was a well-known fact that a room full of monkeys typing randomly would produce the works of Shakespeare, though he was doubtful if this would happen before 5.00 p.m. today.

'Were I a Roman commander,' he intoned, 'I should unsheathe my sword and fall upon its point to save the dishonour of surrender.'

'If you were a Roman commander, and I don't see you making much more than legionary, second class,' a voice behind him said, 'your sword should already be unsheathed and putting the enemy to flight.'

He looked round and saw 'Apple' Charlotte, standing behind him.

'You were talking to yourself and getting it wrong as usual.'

She bent down and kissed him on both cheeks.

'I always like to be symmetrical,' she said.

A slow blush suffused his face; at least suffused is the word he would have used had he been writing. In reality he went bright red. The vacant computer screen mocked him, his only other colleague was pretending not to notice and now Apple, though it was as well not to use that name to her face, was massaging his shoulders. The sensation was very pleasant, but he mustn't let the girl think she could distract him so easily. He tried to devise some articulate, politically relevant, comment. A reference to sexual harassment was a possibility, though the action of Apple's hands was far too exciting to constitute harassment. Did he want her to stop or offer her oblique encouragement? One more try with something deep and political. If that didn't work, he would surrender.

'They should never allow women to serve on nuclear submarines.' He could picture his tutor adding the word, 'Discuss.'

Two sets of nails, decorated in fashionable purple varnish, dug deep into the gap between his collar bone and whatever was below. This was the rib cage, according to the same friendly medic who, he now recalled, had failed anatomy and become a successful bond trader. He flinched but tried not to show it.

'We are not in the control room of a bloody nuclear submarine, you idiot.' The voice was well bred and, despite the edge, soothing.

The nails dug deeper, and he wondered if their owner was trained in lethal unarmed combat and possibly working for the CIA. What interest, however, could that organisation have in a mid-twenties failing journalist who boasted little more than a sophisticated watch and a bulk issue brain?

His confusion was punctured by a hiss of air. Had his lungs been compromised? Apple's voice came in on cue.

'How about inviting me out tonight to an early screening at the Odeon and then a nice Italian dinner?

OK, surrender. 'Tomorrow?'

Apple was adamant – this evening.

'There is one problem,' he said pointing at the blank computer screen.

She cut in. 'A problem already? We can write your article now, a piece about a pleasant evening on the town. I'll dictate it.'

The result was emailed through to the editorial desk. Apple thought it was excellent. She couldn't have put it better herself and fortunately the editor agreed.

A relieved young man sat back, feet on desk, hands behind his head and checked his watch again. Not yet 5.00 p.m. Nothing could go wrong now, unless he forgot himself and called her Granny Smith.

18 September 2012

A Selection of Short, Sometimes Very Short, Stories

Where Did He Go?

The snow was dashing against the car windscreen, half blinding him, as he drove towards the small Cotswold town. His lead was ten, maybe fifteen minutes. No more.

The slippery cobbles seemed to guide him into a parking space just off the High Street. Everything he needed was packed in a small bag ready to be slung over his shoulder.

The street was welcoming as the yellow light from the lamps and shop windows pushed through the snowflakes. Steam came out of the opened doors of the cafes and shops as the customers clutched their parcels and bags and hurried off to their cars.

It would be no more than five minutes now. Should he hide in a shop or mingle with the crowd? Both were too thin to offer much protection.

The police car overshot the turning. Cursing, the driver rammed home reverse, turned, and accelerated down the hill into the town centre.

'Steady,' his partner said as they scraped to a halt.

The driver frowned, removed the safety catch from his pistol and levered himself out of the vehicle.

'Come on,' he yelled. 'He's in here somewhere. He has to be. We both know that all the exit roads are blocked. We'll find him.'

Antiques, bric-à-brac and picture framing looked as good as anything, certainly better than Jane's dresses and maternity wear or the emptying cafes. He pushed at the door and confronted the woman at the counter. She tucked away a wisp of greying hair and adjusted her glasses. The man was agitated as though he was being hunted. She smiled.

'It's cold tonight,' she said quietly. 'You look lost. Can I help you?'

He was burly in his sheepskin jacket, matching his tousled hair and unshaven appearance. The eyes really were blue, the sort you read and dream about. She noted that they darted around all the time, searching desperately.

'That picture in the corner,' he said …

'Is an engraving from the Victorian era,' she replied. 'A very fine example of the genre,' followed automatically by, 'and only a hundred and fifty pounds.'

He pulled a wad of notes from inside his jacket, slapped them on the counter and walked towards the picture. The subject was a village cricket match in front of a big house, probably the vicarage, he guessed.

A plump bewhiskered figure stared out at him, challenged him.

'Fred's just hurt hisself, stupid clot, and we need another fielder. Get some gear on and stand over there.' The man pointed to a position on the boundary.

'Let's try this place,' the driver said. 'It's about the only sizeable premises we haven't examined. Most of 'em are shut,' he added by way of justification to himself.

The two men burst into the antique shop. 'Where is he?' they shouted at the woman.

What rude men. She was glad that she had pushed the money well out of sight beneath the counter.

'Who?'

'Cheeky bitch. No, don't hit her, search the place.'

They blundered through the shop, pulling furniture about and kicking at the heavier items.

'What's this?' The driver said as he held up a sheepskin jacket discarded in a corner.

'That's mine,' the woman said, and then in a gentler voice, 'Please leave it. It gets very cold, and I have to wear it in the shop sometimes.'

The two men turned to one another. 'Some bloated boss who can't be bothered to heat the place properly. It's full of junk. Come on let's go. It's the end of our shift anyway.'

The woman counted the wad of notes again. £5,000. She tried on the jacket. It was a good fit, accommodating her fuller figure. When she wasn't wearing it, it would be an ideal snug for her old cat. He felt the cold terribly now. Then she looked at the engraving. There appeared to be an extra figure in it, standing on the boundary.'

The owner would be very happy indeed with the money. The jacket would keep her warm. The desperate man had been rather good-looking. Muscular, and those eyes. If she hung the picture in her bedroom, when he was bored with the cricket match, he might step out and …

28 October 2009

Sometimes With A Touch of Fantasy/Surrealism

Through A Glass Darkly

The drawing room was spacious, the windows framed by yellow curtains that could be closed to keep out the cold of winter or the light of summer. The chairs, which were upholstered in a matching fabric, had straight backs and uncomfortable seats. Adults admired them and commented on their elegance. Neville pushed the door open slowly and cautiously. He was forbidden to enter this room unless he was being exhibited by his dearest Mama to starched uncles and stout aunts dressed in black, who patted his head and then ignored him. There were many memorabilia of his father's travels scattered around the small tables and the shelves alongside the open, but unlit, fire. One in particular held a fascination for the boy. He picked it up carefully.

'What's that noise?' Captain Queeg pulled blunt fingers through the stubble and salt covering his face. There it was again. It must be a storm coming up. That was it – a storm.

He turned and screamed at the men on the deck. 'Storm. Storm. Furl the sails and splice the main brace. All hands to the pumps and an extra ration of rum.'

Ordinary seaman Ishmael shrugged. 'What an idiot we have for a captain,' he explained to the young midshipman. 'Splicing the main brace is an extra ration of rum.'

The midshipman looked from unfocussed eyes and slowly raised the tin mug to his lips.

A Selection of Short, Sometimes Very Short, Stories

'Sippers, me boy,' Ishmael said. 'Sippers for you lad, not gulpers or you'll be hanging from the yardarm.'

The midshipman, Neville by name, an unhappy youth barely out of spots and into facial hair, still stared in front of him as the alcohol suffused his veins and ran out to his extremities.

'It's like molasses,' he ventured, 'and my dearest Mama said I should sip some molasses every day.'

The captain strode about the deck. 'Wind has dropped,' he observed and, with a telescope clamped to one bloodshot eye, he scanned the horizon.

'Looks like haze in the distance,' he said. As he spun round through the points of the compass, he repeated this information. Until, nor'-nor'-west, over the bowsprit, a dark shape loomed.

'Cliffs,' he yelled. 'Cliffs. Bring her round, helmsman, course forty points south of east.'

The man fought the wheel. 'She's not responding,' he shouted back.

Queeg repaired to his cabin to consult his nautical almanac. He thumbed past port and starboard, bilge pumps and scurvy and back to rudders. That must be it. He stroked his chin again and yelled to the ship's carpenter to check the steering gear.

Neville and Ishmael stood by the wheelhouse. Drink had emboldened the midshipman.

'You know,' he said to Ishmael, 'we're not moving. We are becalmed.' To demonstrate he pulled the older man to the rails. 'Look for yourself. The waves are frozen. Still.'

'Ice,' Ishmael mouthed. And then again, louder, 'We're trapped in the ice. We'll be crushed to death, devoured by the fishes.'

Sometimes With A Touch of Fantasy/Surrealism

A huge hand was clamped to his shoulder. 'Enough, man,' the captain roared in his ear. 'You'll panic the crew. As scurvy a bunch of landlubbers as I ever saw.'

'No, captain.' Ishmael and Queeg looked aghast at the midshipman who had dared to interrupt. 'No,' Neville repeated. 'They can't be a scurvy bunch because they're having lime juice and cabbage every day. That's vitamin C,' he explained knowingly.

Captain Queeg would have flattened the boy had he not been so surprised. As he stared, Neville continued. 'We're not moving because we're stuck inside a bottle. Gordon's gin, I believe.'

'Get the ship's surgeon,' Queeg, Ishmael and the helmsman shouted together.

They looked at one another.

'We don't have one.'

'Then the bosun,' they all said, 'and clamp the boy in irons. He's mad. Raving mad.'

The crash shattered their world as shards of glass rained down on them.

'You stupid child,' his mother said. 'I've told you not to play with that ship in a bottle. Your father will be furious. It was one of his favourite pieces. Now he'll disappear to his study to research his ancestors. Why I married that man, I don't know.'

The eight-year-old looked at the broken remains and for a minute thought he saw something moving. Maybe it was the tears in his eyes.

15 December 2008

A Selection of Short, Sometimes Very Short, Stories

A Murder Mystery

'Sacré bleu, qui es-vous?'

'Nous…'

'English, Watson, English man.' Holmes stepped forward. 'I'll effect the introduction myself. I am Sherlock Holmes, the renowned international detective and this is my assistant Dr Watson.'

The exquisitely sculpted French speaker shrugged his shoulders in the Gallic manner. 'The pleasure of the acquaintanceship is all mine – Mr Shylock Holmes and your amanuensis Doctuer Whats On.'

The three men stood in a comfortably furnished room overlooking the gardens of an Oxford college. Holmes sniffed mightily on a pinch of cocaine and played a few stanzas of Paganini on his Strad.

'Harrumph. This continental mountebank seems to have mistaken me for a Shakespearean character, Watson. He must, I surmise, be Hercule Parrot, that fictional detective.'

'Detective, oui, fictional, non. Poirot, sir, the master Belgian investigateur, the scourge of zee criminal world, at your service.' He touched his scantily covered skull, 'in zere are zee little grey cells zat solve zee mystery.'

Holmes bowed. 'I see, sir, that you have come to these premises by omnibus, that the pavements are wet and strewn with refuse and that you stopped on the way for a cup of hot chocolate topped with cream.'

Amazement showed on the Belgian's face. 'How did you deduce such information?'

Sometimes With A Touch of Fantasy/Surrealism

Watson interrupted. 'It's perfectly simple, my man. Your senior citizen's bus pass is poking out of your top pocket and there are traces of cream and powdered chocolate on your moustache.'

'And the rain, Watson?'

The doctor looked perplexed. He had hoped that Holmes would have failed to notice the omission.

'Observe first, Watson; how many times do I have to tell you? And then deduce. Our friend is immaculate and yet his shoes, finest patent leather, with a mirror like finish, are spotted with water stains and a piece of paper is adhering to the right toe cap.'

Poirot coughed. 'We have been summoned, gentlemen, to investigate a murder and solve it. If not, the reader will be displeased. So where is zee body?'

Holmes walked over to a table under the window and pulled back a sheet to reveal a jumble of whitening bones. 'Voila.'

The other two men joined in the examination.

'Cherchez la femme, 'Watson interjected.

'I believe that you have been reading too many thrillers, Watson, to use the modern terminology. Or perhaps in your case,' Holmes added, 'watching too many theatrical dramatisations. We need to establish and analyse the facts and set up a falsifiable preliminary hypothesis as to what has occurred.'

While this exchange was taking place, Poirot had picked up a rib and was looking at it minutely. He tapped the table with his cane. 'Gentlemen,' he announced solemnly, 'there has been no crime. These bones are plastic and bear the label "Made in China." A student prank, I fear.'

'Alas,' Holmes said, 'There has been a crime, though deception is of a lesser degree than murder. As a

Belgian citizen Monsieur Poirot, you are not entitled to a British senior citizen's bus pass.'

9 July 2008

Sometimes With A Touch of Fantasy/Surrealism

Let's Build A Snowman

The snow lay round about, deep and crisp and even, but motherwife was frazzled. The children were importuning her, begging to investigate the parcels stacked under the tree, and husband was wallowing in a warm bed complaining of a hangover from last night's festivities. In the kitchen the great unwashed – carrots, sprouts and potatoes – and the great unstuffed – turkey – awaited her ministrations.

'Get up, salute the happy morn,' she sang as she flicked the duvet away from her slumbering man, exposing purple pyjamas and white flesh. With ill-concealed grace he tumbled to the floor and assumed his winter woollies. You could never tell with their central heating system. Foredressed was forewarmed.

The family assembled round the breakfast table. Jimmy and his younger sister Cecelia were buzzing with excitement while father was pleading for quiet. They expected a greeting of 'Happy Christmas.' Instead, they were welcomed with plates of steaming porridge. Three stomachs rebelled, anticipating turkey and trimmings much later in the day but, in the end, hunger won and lumps of goodness crashed down the gullet onto the remains of last night's supper. Groans, grunts and belches rent the air as the stressed motherwife apportioned tasks to keep her brood from beneath her feet while she decorated, diced, decocted and cooked.

Duly discharged, man and children retired to the lounge. There was no paper and the battered old TV set was being temperamental, probably because of the indifferent quality of the programmes it was expected to display. Christmas presents represented temptation which must be resisted until after dinner.

Cecelia, an extremely imaginative four-year-old, had convinced her brother that motherwife had a shotgun in the umbrella stand and would use it on the first person to interfere with wrapping paper and ribbon before the appointed time. To clinch the matter, she had reminded him that a large hole had recently been excavated at the back of the garden. It was said that this was to house an oriental fish-pond. Maybe. Grown-ups did not always tell the truth. Father took a more prosaic view. Nevertheless, with motherwife in frazzle mode it paid to be cautious.

Jimmy looked at Cecelia. Cecelia looked at father. Father looked at Jimmy. They all looked at the snow, an endless circle, until, with one voice, they exclaimed, 'Let's build a snowman.'

Wellies joined woollies, gloves covered hands, and hats covered ears as the three adventurers poured forth into the garden screaming and shouting. Snowballs flew, followed by curses, suitably muted, as father was repeatedly hit. As his assailants paused for breath, he assumed senior project manager role.

'You,' he shouted at Jimmy, 'Start shovelling. Cecelia, you start rolling the snow up into a concentric structure.'

'What's concentric?' Cecelia begged of her older brother. He didn't know but using a smidgeon of common sense, something rare in this dysfunctional family, made a guess, a good guess, and soon an obese, seven-foot-high structure appeared as if by spontaneous generation. The children were dispatched

Sometimes With A Touch of Fantasy/Surrealism

to fetch hat, scarf, pipe and sundry vegetables, with which to render the simulacrum more life-like.

The scarf, from a venerable college, was wrapped around the neck of the figure. As no pipe was forthcoming, a lighted Gauloise was slipped between the frozen lips, giving a certain European air to the creation. Onions made the buttons and carrots served their purpose in the pursuit of manly verisimilitude. A glass of steaming grog, from which father surreptitiously supped, was placed within reach of the right hand, and Granddad's bowler used to complete the tableau.

Cecelia innocently and surreptitiously pushed a red pepper into the centre of the frozen mass where she imagined a heart should beat.

The snowman was named Mr Black by a politically aware Jimmy and photographed from all angles, though as father explained, because of the excess of reflected light, all the photographs would be washed out. In reality he had forgotten how to work this damned digital device.

Motherwife, transformed into the snow queen in a glistening gown, sapphire tiara and white sable boots, and thoroughly de-frazzled by the absence of her dearly beloveds and possibly a liberal helping of cooking sherry, came out, inspected and approved. All was forgiven. Though the three might go down with pneumonia or frostbite as a result of their labours, she could face it now.

She bade them to table, where they swapped woolly hats for paper ones and traded excruciating jokes, from the great Chinese joke emporium, as father thrust a two-pronged fork into a bronzed breast, releasing odours and juices to quicken the most jaded appetite.

Jimmy and Cecelia toasted one another in lemonade while motherwife and father resorted to champagne. Flaming plum pudding and custard followed and both Jimmy and Cecelia, by dint of careful parental administrations, avoided swallowing hidden antique half-crowns.

The nuclear family, happily re-fused in harmony, lay round about the glowing hearth, deep and crisp and even. As the children were released upon their presents the snow queen led her snowman off to softer shores where her warmth would melt his heart and possibly reveal a red pepper.

13 December 2007

Sometimes With A Touch of Fantasy/Surrealism

The Sorcerer's Apprentice

'Where's the bloody brief, Sarah?'

'Language, Gordon.'

'Look I've got to explain God knows what to the people tomorrow. I need a brief.'

'Don't worry. We've ten people working on it, four Oxbridge graduates, an American, three working class intellectuals and a woman.'

'That's only nine, Sarah.'

'OK, so maths wasn't my best subject. We could hire a couple of Chinese. They're good at figures.'

The doorbell rings.

'Get it quickly, Gordon, before the children wake up.'

'Why, hello, Alistair. This is a surprise.'

'It shouldn't be, Gordon, you only called earlier this evening and asked me to come round.'

'Of course, Alistair. Could you lend me a few quid, well, make it a few hundred? Some extra bills to pay. I never knew money disappeared so fast.'

'It's all those stealth taxes you introduced, Gordon,' Sarah reminded him.

Gordon mumbles something and frowns.

The phone rings. Gordon dives for the receiver.

'Hello. Nicholas, mon ami, sorry, Monsieur Le President, and you've got Frauline Angela on the line as well.'

Sarah taps her husband's arm and whispers.

'Frau Angela. Look, Nicholas, Entente Cordiale and all that, I'm rather busy at the moment. Can I ring you back tomorrow?'

Holds phone away from ear.

'Foreigners. Can't wait. Wants me to sign up to some treaty giving them the last say on everything. Who won the bloody war?'

'Gordon, I shan't tell you again. No more swearing. And it's Sunday. What would your poor old dad have said?'

Gordon slumps in a chair, with a whisky and soda, picks up a weekend paper and reads his latest ratings. He smiles. 'That's more like it. The people, well, some of them, trust me. I could do with a cigarette, Sarah.'

'I'm afraid not, Gordon. You banned smoking last week.'

He turns to Alistair.

'So, why the midnight call?'

The Chancellor clears his throat.

'It's like this, Prime Minister. I've examined the books and we are, um, up … um, in a mess. The exchequer's going downhill. We're going to need the building societies to prop us up soon, the Europeans are ripping us off, the rain never stops, and people are trying to blow us all up.'

'Not us leaders, surely, Alistair. More likely the ordinary folk.

Sarah fixes him with a stare.

'Oops, sorry, perhaps I got that wrong. The point is, what do we do?'

'My advice, Prime Minister, is to phone George and ask him to send over one or two of his top advisors. They'll soon knock up a convincing scenario.'

The doorbell rings again.

'Tony, good to see you. Sorted the Middle East out yet?'

'Calm down, Gordon. Put on another tie and learn to smile. Remember, I am the Sorcerer and you are my apprentice. You've a lot to learn. You should know by now after thirteen years as my understudy that we are both actors – paid-up members of Equity. The British people haven't elected a politician as Prime Minister for years. They elect actors, some better than others. Each party has its team of script writers, and they knock out a daily offering which may bear some relation to reality, and we have to sell it, ad libbing as we go along. Simple, really. It's a lot easier than being in the real world. All you get there is taxes, no preferential treatment when you go to see the doctor and worst of all you don't know what to say because you haven't got a script to read.'

Gordon gets out of his chair and starts to stride about the room. He is trying to recall a suitable Shakespearean quote. He suddenly turns to Alistair.

'You're not thinking of applying for RADA are you?'

1 July 2007

Note
You can substitute different names if you wish to bring this up to date.

A Selection of Short, Sometimes Very Short, Stories

Janet and John

'Hi, mind if I sit here? The other tables look rather busy.'

She glanced at the man, tall, reasonably dark, and handsome in that overbearing masculine way. The other tables in the bar were not busy but it could be a boring evening sitting here alone with an indifferent paperback – some new writer, and a crossword that she couldn't start.

'Why not?' She started to force a smile and then realised that it was coming naturally.

'I'm John. John Black.' He held out his hand. The hairy wrist disappeared into an immaculately ironed cuff, closed with a heavy monogrammed gold link.

'I'm Mary,' she replied. 'Mary White.'

His grip was strong, if a little lingering.

'Very yin and yang. Would you like another glass of wine?'

Mary noticed that he had that annoying gift some people possess of getting immediate attention from waiters.

While the wine was being uncorked, John appraised Mary White from the top of her blonde head to her elegantly painted toenails, stopping on the way at the faint creases around her eyes, easy figure and long, thin, unadorned fingers. Hardly the little woman. Mary felt his eyes mapping her body and wondered if they could penetrate further than the surface. A pre-emptive strike was needed. She bypassed the weather, contemporary literature, football and anything as crude as politics – attention seekers pursuing their own agenda and calling it democracy.

'What brings you to the heart of rural Warwickshire?' she asked.

Her voice was thick and soothing. You didn't hear what she said, you absorbed it. He imagined himself floating in the words. Then a wave caught him, a quizzical smile built on impatience.

'I'm an investigator.'

'Unsolved murders, secret police, fraud?', though the latter wasn't so interesting, she admitted to herself.

He shook his head, flicked several cashew nuts into the air, caught them in his mouth and smiled for effect.

'Historical,' he replied. 'The real Shakespeare is my present project.'

Mary shifted in her seat, examined a painted toenail short-sightedly – one of her little secrets, sometimes hidden with contact lenses, sometimes revealed with glasses – and recalled her A Level English course.

'I thought that was Marlowe or the Earl of Essex.'

'No. Local grammar schoolboy done good.'

The football accent didn't suit.

'Evidence?'

'Plenty, if you know where to look.' He was serious now. 'Textual, statistical, historical, and, my speciality, immersing oneself in the environment and doing an historical regression.'

'And who pays for you to enjoy yourself?'

As a well-mannered woman she should have regretted the question immediately, but John Black's smugness was beginning to outweigh the potential of his charm as a dinner partner and who knows…

'If you pick the right subject and present your ideas in the right way, there is always a willing paymaster.'

'A rich eccentric, I presume, who probably believes that little green men make crop circles.'

John didn't appreciate the edge of sarcasm. Mary disarmed the blow with a wide smile showing off her even, white teeth.

'I'm sorry, I couldn't resist it. But there isn't that much known about your man, or woman,' she added.

'Are you hungry?' John asked, to get away from the literary impasse.

Mary nodded her head. 'Yes, let's investigate the restaurant.'

She led the way from the distinctly art deco bar to the dated dining room.

'It's rather quaint,' John said. 'How about exploring the town? We might find somewhere possibly mid-twentieth century.'

Mary shook her head and sat down at a table overlooking the street, and beyond that the river. John joined her. She was not a classical beauty, probably approaching forty, and certainly knew her own mind. He would change his approach a little – a decent bottle of wine. What would the Bard have done? Charmed her with words. She didn't top his stories or appear uninterested. Neither did she fall under his spell. She ignored his guidance on the menu, ordered what she wanted to eat, turned down the suggested wine and chatted to the waiter in …

She saw John's confusion. 'Polish, I picked up a little when I was working there.'

Every thrust of his foil was parried by this woman, and she was constantly getting under his guard and scoring hits.

'What were you doing in Poland? Secret agent? Working for Solidarity?'

Sometimes With A Touch of Fantasy/Surrealism

Mary toyed with the latter possibility.

'Do I look that old? she queried. 'Nothing very exciting – I was an au pair girl.'

There was a heavy emphasis on the girl.

John examined her fingers again. There was not even a trace of a light patch amongst the suntan on her ring finger. Neither her clothes or hair or her manner indicated poverty.

He tried again. 'I've got it, you are a clairvoyant. Mystic Mary.'

'That was Meg and if I had been that farsighted, I'd have won the lottery.'

John was not too bad a dinner date. She could examine him more carefully now. Early forties, she guessed, thinning hair, thickening around the waist though well disguised with a nicely cut shirt and comfortable trousers. A would-be family man if he hurried up.

She pushed aside her plate, with its remains of a steak, put her elbows firmly on the table and rested her chin in her linked hands.

'I'm a writer.' She tossed the words out. 'Children's books principally, though I have tried my hand at a novel. You mustn't talk down to children. They want strong characters, and you have to keep up the action. The majority aren't interested in exploring the psyche. The critics don't really enjoy the stories, but my bank manager does. Shall we skip the desserts and just have some coffee?'

John agreed, provided a little brandy was added, and afterwards suggested a stroll by the river. They leant on the parapet of the bridge and gazed into the water, opaque and mysterious. He slid an arm around her shoulders, in a rather tentative, experimental way,

Mary thought. Not what she would have expected from this man.

'No, John,' she said. 'I have something else in mind for you – a family man, happily married and the father of two young children, John Junior, aged seven and Janet, who is nearly nine. You live in colourful suburbia, polish your car on a Sunday morning and after a traditional roast lunch take the family for a walk.'

It was not John Black's idea of life and he suspected, today, no one's idea of life. Perhaps it would be best to enter into her literary world.

'Earlier you said you were a writer. I sound like a character in one of your stories. I'm not certain that I like that. Am I allowed a casual romance while away from home on business?'

He looked at Mary. She was becoming more and more desirable. An evening breeze flicked at her hair and pressed her light dress into the folds of her body. Her perfume was exquisite.

She shook her head. 'Sorry, strictly Boy Scout. The readers would accept no less. Their own lives often hide marital difficulties and troubled offspring and so they want to exist vicariously in a world of make-believe. I could compromise on the lunch – say pasta and salad and make the car a people carrier, but that's all. Come on, I'm getting cold. Let's go back.'

As they walked, John ran the events over in his mind. He had just wanted a pleasant evening, maybe slipping into a night. This delectable woman had out-manoeuvred him. She had been pleasant, but he felt that she had used him – something that rarely happened to him. He shrugged. An early night would do him no harm. And he was a writer. Perhaps he should try to play her at her own game and write the story of John and Mary with the roles reversed. That would be fun.

The hotel lobby welcomed them silently and averted its eyes as they shared a brief goodnight kiss. Mary went to her room, kicked off her shoes, settled in the chair tucked between the radiator and dressing table, and took out her laptop. A quick character sketch – John Black, she would probably change the surname, fortyish, slight plumpness well disguised, thinning on top, a bit of a ladies' man, but a devoted husband and father underneath. She yawned. Slotting him properly into the story could wait until the morning.

It had been a productive evening. She might make it up to him another time in another story.

23 August 2006

A Selection of Short, Sometimes Very Short, Stories

Feeding Charlie

I get up and go to the door, look through the spy hole and open up.

'Hello, Mr Arthurs, how are we?'

It's Doreen, your friendly neighbourhood health care visitor with the royal we. Despite her cheery greeting she looks tired. I smile to encourage her, amble back to my chair, roll up my shirt sleeve and extend my arm.

She takes my pulse and applies the blood pressure monitor.

'Oh,' she exclaims.

I hate that. You don't know whether it's good or bad. It's obvious why she visits the old'uns, like me. The practice wants to keep the books straight and know when any of us pop off. It's called health care management. Just because we are old doesn't mean we're stupid.

She could do something useful and stay for a cup of tea and a talk. Tell me about the problems with her latest boyfriend. She may be in her forties, but she still has problems with boyfriends or, as she puts it, with men and relationships. I might be able to help. I ask her to stay but she shakes her head.

'Sorry, Mr Arthurs, not today. Must nip along now, see you next month. I'll let myself out.'

Efficient madam. The door slams and I'm on my own again.

I'd like to tell you a bit more about my life. It won't make any difference to the world, but it will make me

Sometimes With A Touch Of Fantasy/Surrealism

happy to let you into some of my secrets.

I'm one of the billions of ordinary folk. We come, we go, we pay our taxes. We disappear and are forgotten. No monuments for us. No obituaries. We've never been famous soldiers or politicians or leaders, just the PBI.

I've lived in this semi-detached villa for fifty-one years. These villas used to be exclusive, facing countryside and woods. Not now, since they deposited thousands more houses around us. I mustn't complain though.

Before I fade away for ever, let me amuse you with a few of my stories. I'll start with my special friend, Charlie. He was a big fellow. Black hair, heavy shoulders and yellow eyes with a vertical slit in the centre. I used to swear at him if I saw him stalking in our garden. From inside the house, you understand. People in our road never swore outside – far too proper. That's changed now. Some of the kids round here can't even pronounce their own name without a– I won't bother you with that.

I used to feed Charlie, on and off, for years. When his owners were away. It was no trouble. He got very lonely, rubbed around your legs and meowed. One morning he was so miserable that I squatted down on the floor, looked into his eyes and tried an experiment. I meowed back. Charlie was so surprised that he opened his mouth so wide I could see daylight at the other end.

That reminds me – you've time for a digression or two I hope? – of when I was eleven or twelve. We had this biology teacher.

'Boy,' she said to me one day, 'Do you know what you are? And that goes for the rest of you.'

She looked around the whole class.

'A hollow tube. Food goes in one end and comes out of the other' – she must have heard about me and the unripe plums I pinched. 'Attached to the top end is your control box, your brain, only in your case there isn't much there.'

She looked hard at me.

'You've legs for running about and arms for poking around with. And a backbone. That has two uses. To support your interior organs – a pump and a few other floppy bits – like washing on a clothesline and to stop you collapsing in a heap on the floor.'

I mumbled, 'Yes, Miss.'

It seemed the safest thing to do. I remember that she never mentioned sex, but then you didn't in those days. It was called reproduction and it only happened if you were married, though there were one or two cases, spoken of in hushed tones, where something had gone wrong.

My throat is quite dry with all this talking. I'll make myself a cup of tea and then I'll tell you some more about Charlie. You're not bored, are you? You won't go away? Where was I? Talking to Charlie. I tried tonal variations on meow. Like high pitched meowing and deep bass stuff. It's the way the Chinese speak. They don't meow, of course but they are always varying the pitch. I know that because in the war I met this Chinese girl. A serene face and gorgeous black eyes that would suck your soul out when you were making love. I don't think I ever recovered mine properly. I moved on and married Elsie when I came home. She was a bit antiseptic. We had two children. I hear from them at Christmas, but they never come to visit. Probably fed up with my stories.

Sometimes With A Touch of Fantasy/Surrealism

To get back to Charlie. Tonal variations proved very successful in talking to him. We had long conversations. It turned out he was interested in words. I was doing a prize crossword one day and thoroughly stuck. I was talking to myself while feeding him and I happened to meow the clue, and he meowed back, 'rebarbative'. I was quite surprised because it fitted perfectly, I'd never heard of the word before, and I won a consolation prize in the competition.

After a few drinks to celebrate I mentioned it to Elsie – crosswords and Charlie and all that. She went very quiet, touched her face a lot and asked when I had last changed my socks. Next birthday she bought me the Oxford Shorter Dictionary. That's two pretty hefty volumes. It surprised me because she was never much of a reader.

I was consulting it one evening when N to Z plus the addendum slipped from my hands and landed on my foot. I went to see the doctor the day after.

Synthetic smile for next patient.

'What can I do for you?'

'I've dropped a dictionary on my foot,' I began.

'Novel.'

'No dictionary, the Oxford Shorter, Volume Two.'

He was writing quickly by then.

'Take these twice a day and you'll soon be all right.'

As I left, I think I heard him mutter, 'The foot anyway.'

The power of words and the scope for misunderstanding is frightening. What if I'd had a pain in my stomach and he had said appendix and I had replied Chapter Two? I could have died.

He's long gone to the golf course, but I think he must have passed my details on. It's the way they back off when I appear at the surgery and say I'll be fine before I've listed all my symptoms.

Eventually, poor old Charlie succumbed. He had been going downhill for a couple of years – bits of his nose kept falling off. One night he curled up in his favourite chair and when his owners looked in on him in the morning, he was stiff – deceased, as they say.

The two young boys living on the other side took it badly. They insisted on making him a coffin from shoe boxes and giving him a military funeral. They fired their water pistols over the grave. Caught Elsie in the eye but she didn't mind. It was one of her good days.

I've often pondered, um, on decomposition. I know it's not nice to talk about, but it happens to us all one way or another. We are all made up of atoms, mainly, if I remember, carbon and water – I used to be good at chemistry at school. There are lots of trace elements as well. You only have to look at a packet of vitamin and mineral pills to see how many. Then there are all those artificial things that they make in America. I've read about them. They only exist for a billionth of a second, so you'd hardly expect to find any of those in the average body. The point is that all these atoms are returned to mother earth in one way or another. If he had been cremated, you could be breathing parts of Charlie, or anyone else, I suppose. It might be someone you really disliked. Then they really would be getting up your nose.

A new vicar called on me one day a few years ago. Perhaps he smelt a conversion. I expect he had targets like everyone else. We chatted over a cup of tea. He asked me where my wife was, and I told him that she had died last year. He said he was sorry to hear that and then I said, could I ask him a question?

He smiled. 'Of course.'

'Vicar, just suppose those home-grown broad beans I've had for lunch had somehow been imbued with some atoms from my Elsie. Would that be cannibalism?'

He looked a bit alarmed, so I explained that I had scattered her ashes on the vegetable patch. That didn't seem to reassure him either. He swallowed hard, hooked a finger into his dog collar, said Jesus loves you and disappeared.

He's never been back. I would like to have had another talk to him. Perhaps cannibalism was the wrong word, but I don't think that that made a real difference. He just hadn't been trained for my sort of question in his apprenticeship.

What's that noise? Oh, it's Jenny coming in. I've forgotten to mention her. She only appeared on the scene last year. She's black like Charlie but she lives with me, not next door. Very loving but also an independent miss. It's her terms or none.

I expect you don't believe all my stories. Lots of people say I embroider things a bit. Doreen called in the other evening. Not one of her regular visits. She looked awkward as well as tired. I wondered if she made the wrong measurements on me last time and received a rocket from the boss. Then I looked again and saw it was far too serious for that.

'Mr Arthurs.'

She hesitated, bit her lower lip and started to blush and then,

'Could I have a word with Jenny, please?'

She wouldn't look at me directly.

'Of course.'

She went over to the cat and stroked her head. Jenny purred and her body started to vibrate. Then I saw

Doreen whispering in a furry ear. Now I understood. She wanted advice, probably about her latest man. Nothing came of it. Jenny got bored and wandered off to see what was in her supper dish.

Doreen looked at me accusingly.

'You told me often that your cats talked.'

I had to correct her. I'm a bit pedantic.

'The cat I used to look after, that's Charlie, talked a lot, but it takes a long time to build up, what do you call it, a trusting relationship. You can't go up to any old moggy and say, evening, I've a bit of a problem, what do you think I can do about it? And besides, female cats are pretty reserved about personal matters.'

She looked so crestfallen. I asked her if she would like a cup of tea. This time she accepted. I even found some biscuits. Probably past their sell-by date, though they still tasted good. We sat on my old sofa and for once I was listening and someone else was talking. She said I had eased her mind and when she left, she closed the door quietly.

13 September 2003 and 18 February 2004

Sometimes With A Touch of Fantasy/Surrealism

The Public Library – A Romance In One Volume

The wooden cross was gently cradled by the more intimate and ample folds of Mavourine Magruder's body and hidden today from hurtful stare by a green silk blouse. The edges of the wood were rounded and the surface polished to a fine patina. A constant supply of garlic cloves macerating amongst her teeth added reinforcement. The refined pearl choker disguised a stab proof light-weight neck protector. She had, reluctantly, given up the chain mail shirt on her doctor's advice; before her shoulders and spine were permanently deformed by the weight. Her final line of defence was a stake, with a fire hardened point, and a 7lb hammer nestling within easy reach beneath the library service desk. The hammer had proved so heavy that she had been obliged to enrol at the local gym to improve her biceps. It was all worth it, she knew. Only a very foolhardy vampire would dare try to attack her now.

The local council was entirely happy with the slightly eccentric Miss Magruder. Few people went near the library. Those that ventured inside either inserted plugs of cotton wool into their nostrils or rushed out into the street on the completion of their business to gulp in lungfuls of pollution. The council didn't have to hire additional assistants, the computers were rarely used, and the purchase of new books and magazines was minimal. Best of all, the cultural directorate of the EU could be assured that adequate provision had been made for the literary needs of the local population and the government that all their targets had been met.

Despite her lack of customers, the librarian was never idle. The books, or rather the individual letters, were a constant worry. Lower case hs were among the most troublesome – always trying to sneak away. Mavourine herself thought, and she was sure most responsible citizens would agree with her, that the upper-case letters should set a better example. Not so. As and Xs were particularly irresponsible. She could understand that Xs, being at the end of the alphabet and not widely used, perhaps felt themselves to be second class letters, though she had pointed out to them that they stood as a cipher for love. But As. She despaired. With such adult behaviour it was not surprising that youth sometimes strayed. Ks and ks, especially in books by Australian authors, were especially skittish, as if infected by some antipodean anarchism. The worst letters, were, however, Os of any age. They were a menace because they would roll out into the street. If too many escaped, people could be upended en masse and that would be so dangerous for the old and infirm, or even very tall people with brittle bones. It was a constant battle to keep the books readable and the streets safe. Nobody knew of her struggles, and nobody would care if they did, she reflected with sadness. To comfort herself she recalled her mother's words, quoted on many different occasions. 'Such is the burden of service placed on the gentler sex'.

'Good morning, how are you?'

A man, leaning across the counter and smiling at her, had uttered these startling words in a leisurely manner. Miss Magruder appraised him with care, her hand ready to grab stake and hammer. He was tall, with glasses and an unobtrusive hearing aid. A man was a man, despite her mother's warning that all such creatures were the spawn of the devil. The librarian pushed this thought aside, noticed his worn, wobbling and stained teeth, wondered if any other parts of his body were enhanced by prosthetic additions, concluded that they were not and smiled back.

'Good morning. How may I help you?'

As she spoke, she hastily pushed Os and os aside in case his bones were brittle and he should trip.

'I wonder if I could look at your tape library?' he asked.

She ushered him to the section, hovered and then left to chase more letters.

Robert Romero had led a sheltered life. He was therefore surprised to find that all the tapes were pre-recorded. It was a blank one that he required. He had been instructed by a higher authority to record onto a blank tape that night in order that the mysterious voice of the Great One could inform him on what to do next to save humanity. He counted out the amount of money left from the purchase of his tape recorder, remembered that he must get groceries and concluded that it was a pre-recorded tape or nothing. He selected an abridged version of Gibbons' *Decline and Fall*, that ran to a mere sixteen cassettes, and approached the check-out desk. Customers, especially men rarely smiled at her and Miss Magruder had taken the opportunity to fluff her red streaked blonde hair and apply some lipstick. She registered his loan in the computer, which was perhaps more surprised than she at the action, and wished the gentleman a nice day.

Back in his flat, Mr Romero turned his attention and a small screwdriver to the tape cassettes. By inserting and twisting where it said in bold letters 'Do Not Touch' he was able to break the clip preventing over-recording. After a substantial supper and half a bottle of a rather good Burgundy he retired to his bed, loaded and set the recorder, switched it on and waited. The wine quickly dulled his senses, he started to mutter and snore, and then his left hand crashed onto the off switch of the recorder.

Awaking refreshed at 6.33 a.m. he recalled his vivid dream. The Great One had told him what to do next. He was to begin expunging all prepositions from books and documents. When other dedicated members had been recruited to MI7, so secret that no one knew of its existence, apart from Robert Romero, the task would extend to adverbs, verbs, nouns and adjectives. With written communication removed from the world, the next step would be to set about the spoken word. If this could be eliminated, Mr Romero was assured, conflict would be a thing of the past. People would only be able to communicate by grunting, thus constraining all politicians and bureaucrats, and world peace would ensue. As a bonus, members of MI7 would be the leaders of the new order.

There was no need for tapes now. Mr Romero retraced his steps to the library and a delighted Miss Magruder was again startled with:

'Good morning, how are you today?'

The man smiled, thanked her profusely for her help, smiled again and left. It was, he decided, rather unfair to start removing prepositions from library books after the generous welcome that he had received there. He would purchase a paperback and start on that. Later he might graduate to the library.

And then the fates, forever toying with man's destiny, and in this case woman's, came into play. Intemperate weather in Mexico combined with a distribution strike in Great Britain caused a temporary hiatus in garlic supplies and Mr Romeo became immersed in the story from which he was supposed to be removing all prepositions. Miss Magruder found no increase in the potential vampire population, and became so enthralled with ordinary day-to-day chit chat with new friends and visitors to the library that she forswore the bulb, though she did take the precaution of swallowing a handful of odourless garlic pills with her breakfast tea to keep her blood ever virginal. Even the escaping letters ceased to bother her. Perhaps it had all been a minor brain disturbance.

Mr Romero had chosen a torrid love story to read and work on, rejected by thirty-four publishers before spiralling to success, so he was assured one morning by his newspaper. He so identified with the hero that he resigned from MI7, turned his back on the Great One and sought love instead. That was not, he found, an easy commodity to come by. Having finished the paperback, he called in at the library one afternoon for further supplies to stimulate his imagination and reinforce his hope.

'Good afternoon. How may I help you?' Miss Magruder smiled and spread her hands in welcome.

'Come on, old man, go for it.' The voice was similar to that of the Great One, but livelier and more encouraging. He smiled back, cleared his throat, twice, swallowed and, as he felt the beads of sweat forming on his forehead, managed to speak.

'There's a very well thought of film showing at the cinema tonight. I wondered if you would, ah, um, like to accompany me?'

There, it was out. He could breathe again.

He waited while she swelled with anticipation and managed to produce a comely, 'Yes' and then a ladylike, 'Delighted,' when her soul wanted to scream, 'Yes please.'

The Odeon yielded two of its best seats to Mr. Romero's wallet and entertained the couple, though not to the extent indicated by the anonymous reviewer. The film was short and Mr Romero, who had not been able to eat all day, was now hungry.

He steeled himself again.

'How about a glass of wine and something to eat at that new Italian place in the High Street?' he asked.

Miss Magruder considered the proposal for a moment, out of politeness, before agreeing enthusiastically.

The restaurant welcomed them with a table for two with a view of the busy street outside.

'Yes, I'll have a small glass of red wine, please – nothing too heady. Oh dear, do I mean heavy?'

The waiter smiled because he knew that the same bottle would produce heavy, soft, light, medium or dry, depending on the diner's wishes.

'And to eat, madam?'

A lengthy exploration of the menu suggested mountain-dried ham, salad and crusty garlic bread. The couple chatted and sipped sufficient wine to make a refill necessary.

'Do you like braised aubergines and Mahler?' she enquired.

'Yes,' he replied, 'but not together,' thus pre-empting the confusion beginning to flood her body at her attempt at intelligent small talk.

Over dessert, sweet or pudding, depending on one's pretensions, Mavourine, for the names were intimate now, sought a safer topic of conversation than food and music and mentioned to Robert the strange tale of the damaged tapes. Silence.

Robert played with his spoon and carved his crème caramel into exotic shapes.

'It was I,' he admitted and poured out the whole sordid tale.

Forgiveness was immediate.

They walked back to her house untroubled, until testosterone triumphed, and Robert tore the wooden cross from its warm and comfortable residence behind a blue silk blouse and showered it with kisses before gently replacing it.

Frightened by his own daring, Robert bent down and plucked a handful of lilies of the valley to offer as a reparation for his behaviour and to show the gentler, feminine, side of his nature.

Still throbbing with delight, Mavourine sucked in their scent.

'Beautiful,' she murmured.

Robert merely nodded and then made another confession.

'I'm afraid I have absolutely no sense of smell. Never have,' he emphasised.

That didn't matter, she thought. He presumably retained the other four.

14 March 2004

A Selection of Short, Sometimes Very Short, Stories

What Did I Say?

'… and I've served my time helping humanity – five months in med school,' I said.

'How interesting.'

My hostess tried to hide a yawn with a be-ringed hand, and I noticed that her eyes were beginning to glaze over.

'There's someone I want you to meet,' she said as she grabbed my arm and pulled me through the talking, drinking groups that filled her ample sitting room and spilt out into the garden. Our path seemed somewhat erratic, and I detected desperation in her movement.

'Julia,' she shouted as she saw a slim, dark-haired girl entering the room, 'I want you to meet Robert.'

The introduction was precise and breathless. 'Robert is a part-time taxidermist and sculptor and,' she whispered in my ear as she disappeared, 'Julia specialises in assassinations.'

As our hands touched briefly and we exchanged the customary 'hellos', I assessed my fellow guest. Nearer 30 than 20. Medium height. A brown band of sun-tanned skin acted as a boundary between her tight black trousers and simple white top. And violet eyes. My antennae should have alerted me, but the early warning system was totally disabled by sight, sound and scent. We smiled and both moved instinctively towards the drinks, and then into the garden to escape from the reverberating noise.

'Phew, that's better,' I said.

Sometimes With A Touch of Fantasy/Surrealism

She nodded, we sipped the surprisingly good champagne and she asked, 'are you a friend of the bride or groom?'

I shook my head and frowned with puzzlement. Was I at the wrong party? She laughed and showed her very even, very white teeth.

'Sorry, I shouldn't have tried to throw you like that. I know this is just a summer do. It's professional interest. I probe inside peoples' minds, pull out the tangled skeins of thoughts and emotions, unknot them and push them back. It's called psychiatry,' she added by way of an explanation.

I took too deep a gulp of champagne and started to choke. As a reward I was thumped between the shoulders and pulled to a nearby garden bench to recover. With the score at fifteen love, she pressed home her advantage.

'You know, Robert, you don't look to me as though you could stuff a lost wax bronze casting if you tried. What do you really do?'

This was rapidly turning into a rout. I studied my feet, fingernails, and a lot more of Julia.

'I, I am a tax inspector – junior grade.' I finally pushed the words out and stopped with a deep sigh. She grinned at me.

'It could be worse; it might be double-glazing. Come on, cheer up, let's find something to eat.'

We returned to our bench with laden plates.

'Do you like pepperoni?' Julia asked as she offered me a piece she had removed with distaste from her pizza.

'Love it.' I swallowed it quickly and reciprocated with anchovy.

Here were the makings of compatibility.

'What about kidney?' I asked her.

'Hate the things,' she shot back.

'So do I. We'll avoid pies from now on.'

She nodded in agreement. We continued exploring our personae over drinks and coffee and finally parted, at her place, early in the morning.

She had a heavy work schedule, she said, and it would be a week before we could meet up again. I invested in new shirts and shower gel, found the vacuum cleaner, had my hair cut. My flat mate remarked that, 'I had it bad again.'

The phone call came on Friday night.

'Hi, how are you doing?' was the most original thing I could think of as my carefully rehearsed phrases evaporated in my brain.

'Come along to the departmental thrash on Saturday night and meet some friends,' was her reply. It sounded harmless enough. I agonised about a shark's tooth necklace or a medallion. Friends remarked, passé, or out of fashion even before you were born, so I abandoned the idea and went unadorned.

Julia had a hand wrapped around a glass of vodka, probably diluted with more of the same. Polka dots of brown flesh peeped out from her lace dress. The violet irises were sliding into blue, and her skin was iridescent. She was talking intently to a distinguished looking man in a pin stripe suit. The boss, I surmised.

'I'll be with you in a minute,' Julia called over her shoulder as she continued chatting away.

I decided to lower my inhibition level with some alcohol.

'White wine, please.'

I tried to remember an appropriate grape, but the barman was impatient.

Sometimes With A Touch of Fantasy/Surrealism

'Sweet or dry, mate?'

To pass the few minutes until Julia was free, I strolled over to a row of paintings on a far wall.

'Picasso,' the man next to me announced.

'Looks as though the perspective is a bit dodgy,' I replied. That unerring instinct that some of us possess some of the time flashed up, 'Careful.'

'What did you say?' The man's voice was stilted now, and the delivery deliberate. He turned to face me. His staring eyes drilled through, pinning me to the wall. I could feel the screws being driven home. One last turn and the job would be complete. It was probably topped off with a builder's guarantee.

A matronly woman on my right whispered, 'Watch out, he's a nutter.'

One side of my brain told the other to stop fantasising about the sinuous body and sensuous mind I was supposed to be escorting tonight and which seemed just beyond my consummation. One more false step and it would be so for ever.

Autospeak took over.

'You misunderstood what I was trying to say,' I waffled. 'Picasso is the seminal exponent of visual change in the twentieth century. We can all imitate, only genius can initiate.'

This sounded so good I was beginning to believe my own opinions. The man seemed to be taking my words into his mouth, chewing and tasting them slowly before, I hoped, swallowing.

No, not really, I realised. This was definitely not going to be a civilised discussion. He was closing down my personal space and his hands were slowly rising towards my throat. Specks of saliva flecked his lips and chin.

133

A slim hand, with clear varnished nails, appeared on his right shoulder and pushed him gently away from me. A sweet, disarming smile gazed at him as the toe of a black, lightweight, graceful size 7 arced into his crotch. I saw his lips part, as if to challenge my artistic judgement again, the eyes come unstuck and roll upwards and the knees buckle all in a flowing, undifferentiated movement. He sank without trace.

Julia shrugged. 'Always works. Better than Prozac, on men anyway,' she added in a technical aside. 'Sorry, I was busy when you came in.' She used her most artless smile to illuminate my face. 'I have to secure funding for next year, and', she shrugged casually, 'men are so susceptible to rational argument at the right moment. Let's dance.'

It was an order, not to be disobeyed. She pulled me into the small, reserved, space.

Her body exhibited the best example of organised chaotic motion I had ever witnessed. Computer generated graphics became a fading memory. Julia flung her head back. Her eyes were unfocussed and her mouth half open. Her short dress began to ride up invitingly over her thighs. I struggled to move my feet fast enough. My emotions were already outpaced.

We lay together in the blackness, holding each other, exhausted. Her scent and feel were overwhelming my brain, but I tried to tease the thought out of the back of my mind. I went back for a couple of decades. I must have been eleven, twelve? Biology one. I could picture the teacher. Very pretty, sadistic.

'Boy, pay attention. Do you know what spiders do after they have mated?' A ripple of suppressed grins.

'No, miss.'

'The female eats the male.'

I felt Julia's lips touch my shoulder. Maybe it was just my genes she wanted. I could offer no resistance.

19 July 2001

A Selection of Short, Sometimes Very Short, Stories

The House of Dreams

'World War Three just broke out', the crackling voice announced over the radio. 'South of the town, big house by the reservoir.'

Joe spat coffee, burger, boredom and cigarette through the car window and tossed Kierkegaard aside. He knew the place. There was only one house down there. He was touching seventy as he rode through the third set of red lights.

He flicked the switch on the radio. 'Any back-up?' he enquired.

'Yeah,' came the bored voice, 'Herb.'

Joe cheered wildly and pounded the steering wheel with both fists. Herb Ezekiel was scrawny but shrewd. This was going to be his night.

He turned off the potholed road, slewed his car round onto a mixture of gravel and disused flower beds, and nearly demolished a decaying porch. He seemed to burst out of the car and rolled over on his side to the dark entrance. The occasional sting of stone or thorn went unnoticed. The heavy wooden door, with discoloured brass fittings, swung open noiselessly with the push of a finger. That never happened in real life. Too easy. He loosened his gun and flung a stun grenade down the hallway. Crouching and covering his ears, he waited for the explosion to subside and then charged. The room appeared to stretch forever in all directions. For someone brought up in a semi, this was a definition of spacious.

Sometimes With A Touch of Fantasy/Surrealism

'Good evening. I believe that is the customary welcome, even to one as impetuous as yourself.'

The darkness and the frenzy in Joe's brain slowly cleared together. A quiet, cultured voice was the last thing he'd expected to hear. Joe scanned the room again, the peeling wallpaper, the old-fashioned cast-iron radiators. He noted the dying Roman legionnaire. Blood was spurting from the gaps between the bronze armour plates on his chest, then disappearing into the sand.

'Don't you acknowledge a greeting?' It was the same voice that had spoken when he entered the room. Laughing now.

Joe forced his gaze to concentrate on the centre of the room. There was the voice. A bleached white skeleton lounging on a pile of ammunition boxes. The eyes glowed green from the depths of the skull. The teeth were clamped around a cigar of generous girth. On each intake of breath smoke seeped out of the ribcage. A slender hand pulled a golden crown down until the rim nearly covered the eyes.

'You must be The Joker,' Joe observed.

'At your service.' The gesture was elegant but not servile.

'Let me ask you a question.'

'Of course,' the Joker replied.

Joe hesitated while he formulated his thoughts. 'That Roman soldier, is he real or a waxwork figure? He looks like a picture I saw in a book once.'

The Joker smiled, that is if you can smile with no lips.

'It's up to you to decide, Joe. Is all this real or are you creating it, or remembering it?'

In an enthusiastic burst of self-improvement, Joe had been attending philosophy classes one evening a week for four weeks now. He ran a quick mental review. Mainly it seemed to be about doubting everything, especially your assumptions, and then arguing endlessly using long words he didn't understand. In the dark light of a nightmare, it was no help at all.

'I'm waiting for an answer, Joe. Stuck. Let's try something else.'

A bearded Viking axeman strode into the room and through the swirling dust the scared hull of a tank clashed with a chariot. As Joe watched he was aware of somebody behind him. He couldn't turn and was unsurprised at the tap on his shoulder. Then his legs began to falter. The arms that caught him were surprisingly strong for such a small man.

Herb Ezekiel pulled him into a trench.

'Those were solid floorboards a minute ago,' Joe protested as he brushed earth off his clothes.

Herb put his hands on Joe's shoulders and forced him to squat on a kitbag.

'You confused?' he asked the younger man gently.

'No. Yes. I don't know. Totally. There was never anything like this in training,' Joe began. 'There were good guys and bad guys and weak guys, but they often counted as bad, and they all tried to beat hell out of you, and,' he paused, 'they were never polite and they didn't ask you crazy questions, just screamed they were innocent.'

'Have a cigarette.'

Herb lit two and pushed one between Joe's lips.

'How about a drink?'

'On duty?' Joe, the older man queried with a smile.

'Forget that, survival is all that counts here.'

'There's no noise, no stench,' Joe muttered. 'It's all visual.'

Herb pushed his fingers through his tight curly hair before he answered.

'Different people get it in different ways. Then, sometimes he changes the rules.'

'How did I know he is called The Joker?' Joe was ferreting away, desperate for anything that made sense.

'He gets into your mind,' Herb replied, 'but mainly for his amusement. He likes to see people react. Then he pushes you aside. And don't think of using that,' Herb said as Joe grasped his gun. 'It won't work in here and it might just annoy him and…' He shook his head.

The two men peered over the parapet of the trench. All that remained in the clear air of a rather nondescript, shabby, furnitureless lounge, was a pair of fading green emeralds, about the same distance apart as a man's eyes.

'I'm leaving you now. That's enough back-up for one day. Take your time, Joe and keep this to yourself.'

Joe rubbed the back of his hand across his forehead. He was thirsty and tired and disoriented. The wall bulged slightly. Something moved underneath the peeling paper. A hand broke through into the room, next a face. A beautiful woman slowly formed. She was straight out of an advertising hoarding. She shook her black hair to free it, peeled away her clothes and smiled very gently at him.

'Don't be scared, Joe.'

She pulled him towards her.

He shivered and gagged in the cold breeze, scudding off the water. He pulled his jacket around him and pressed his back into the outer wall of the house. The moonlight was steel grey. It hit him in the face. Joe looked up and saw the wooden sign, hanging askew over the door. From the peeling paint he reconstructed the legend, 'The House of Dreams.'

The linen was hard, white, and cool. Joe was propped up in a metal bed. The room was dimly lit and yellow. The young female orderly monitored his pulse and blood pressure in a very businesslike way.
 'Can I have more light?' Joe asked.
 She shook her head. 'Not in your state, young man.'
 Did she think he was a baby? Should he tell her? No one would believe him. It was like Herb would have said, 'Best keep it to yourself.'

19 June 2001 and 8 July 2002

Sometimes With A Touch of Fantasy/Surrealism

Margarine

The kitchen and adjoining breakfast room passed a peaceful night. As the low sun began to shine through the orange blinds, the house woke up to the bumps and groans of the central heating system. The wife abandoned the warmth of her bed for her first duty of the day – the organisation and despatch of her family to their appointed destinations. Two of those were school. Her husband's could be more problematical. She pushed these thoughts aside as she laid four places at the round wooden table. Since she never knew what her family would have until they were in place, she put down a generous assortment of utensils, plates, bowls, cup, saucers and mugs. She poured herself her first cup of coffee of the day and waited.

'Could you get another pack of butter from the fridge, please,' she shouted across to her son as she heard him crash into the kitchen.

'What, Mum?'

'Oh, never mind, I might as well do it myself.'

The boy, fourteen years old, lanky and untidy, with his mobile phone pressed to one ear, handed her the carton of margarine. He grinned. 'Just testing, Mum. Remember, we don't have butter anymore, not after Dad's cholesterol scare.'

'How could I forget? How could anyone in this house forget? He never does. It'll drive me mad.'

'But you still love him, don't you?' her daughter enquired.

'Of course,' Mother replied, giving her nine-year-old a big hug.

The table was rapidly being covered with spilled food and drink. Was there some universal law of attraction between milk, tea, coffee and cereals and clean surfaces? Or perhaps a genetic predisposition within her family making them messy eaters? It could be both, of course. These philosophical musings were suddenly shattered.

'Morning, everyone.' Dad appeared in his, "I'm going to an important meeting" mode. Best suit, polished black shoes, matching socks, rumpled shirt, tie askew and raging panic. He inserted himself in the family group, nearly upsetting the orange juice and knocking both his spoon and knife to the floor. He picked up his daughter's serviette and made a wild grab for the paper.

'What would you like to eat? his wife asked very calmly.

'I haven't really got time. Cup of tea, cereal. Yes. No. All right. Any skimmed milk?'

'It's low on calcium, Dad,' his son interjected, 'and that means brittle bones.'

Mother frowned at her son. 'That's not Dad's problem today.'

'I'll have some toast,' he announced, grabbing a piece resting on the edge of his daughter's plate.

'Butter, marge I mean,' he said stretching across the table to get the unopened packet.

It was a new brand, low in everything except price. The packet bore the legend 500g e.

'What the hell does that mean?' Dad asked everyone.

Mother and daughter started talking at the same time. The former questioning his need for profanity this early in the morning, the latter to explain about the EU and selling things in grams and not pounds, 'Which we all understand,' he snorted.

Dad tugged at the lid. When he had opened the packet, he was faced with a layer of gold coloured foil 'which sealed the goodness in and kept the germs out,' his daughter said. After a few experimental prods with the bread knife, he succeeded in letting the germs in and goodness out. He looked at the smooth, yellow surface.

'It looks quite virginal,' he mused, panicking so much he forgot he was in a hurry.

Daughter looked at Mother, puzzled.

'He means it's undisturbed, dear,' the latter explained quickly.

Then father smelt it. Nothing. Well, maybe a faint odour of butter. Finally, he removed a smidgen on his knife to do the taste test. OK.

His daughter had lost her toast and was suddenly bored. She seized the pristine pack of margarine from her father, stuck her knife in it up to the hilt and exclaimed, 'Excalibur.'

'Don't be stupid,' her brother yelled at her, 'you only say that when you pull the sword out.'

The girl started to cry and kicked her brother under the table. As retaliation and a general state of hostilities seemed inevitable, Mother physically separated the warring parties, whispered something in her son's ear and asked her daughter where she had heard the story of King Arthur and the sword.

By now Dad had reduced his panic level by a quantum leap and proceeded to spread margarine on his slice of toast with a maniacal thoroughness, leaving no corner of the hardened bread untouched.

'Spreads well,' he observed as he ladled on his wife's home-made lemon marmalade.

'Do you mean the butter which is really marge, or the marmalade?' his son enquired. 'Or maybe the toast itself, which by its nature cannot spread?' The male members of the family were about to debate the correctness of these statements at length and probably with considerable violence, when Mother, smiling sweetly through clenched teeth, propelled her son towards the door, and saw him off with, 'Have you got your sports gear?'

She knew from experience that the nod he gave her might mean,'yes, no, I'm not bothered, or 'Mind your own business.'

The putative head of the house was now icily calm, having been 'tead' and 'toasted', and he smiled at his wife.

'Phew, you keep things running so well, you should be in politics.'

'I am,' she replied. 'This is the sharp end. That lot at Westminster wouldn't last ten minutes here.'

Her husband gathered up his papers and coat and was despatched to his meeting. Her daughter was pointed in the direction of school. Finally, Mother could have some time to herself. She could sit at the breakfast table and relax with the paper, toast and a second cup of coffee before solving the next crisis. She caught sight of the mangled and polluted surface of the margarine, covered with black specs of burnt bread, marmalade and worse. She shuddered and reached behind her chair, into a cupboard, and brought out her secret supply of unsalted, Normandy, butter. Bliss.

1 March 2001 and 8 July 2002

Vaguely Biblical?

A Selection of Short, Sometimes Very Short, Stories

Clothes Doth A (Wo)man Make

He was a hunky chunk, he ploughed and sowed and reaped and mowed but something was lacking in his life.

Female companionship. Evie, who lived in the big house at the top of the hill, was his ideal.

He went to see a man of the cloth to explain his predicament. 'Clothes my boy, clothes,' he was told, 'they doth a man maketh.'

This was a revelation (appropriate coming from a man of the cloth). Our hunky chunk had always treated sunburn and sleet with equal indifference. Now he knew more was needed.

He consulted the internet and ordered a Lincoln green, organic fig leaf, described as covering all eventualities.

He chanced upon Evie one day in the village shop. 'Would you care,' he asked her, 'to take a drink with me this evening in the Bullrush and Basket?'

Being a well brought-up young woman, she blushed, lowered her eyes and shook her head. 'Sire,' she replied, 'many a young maiden has repaired to that establishment only to return with something to fill her basket.'

'How about the Camel and Driver, then?' (There being no horses and jockeys at that time in that place.)

She agreed. Sitting at a table, she with her apple juice and he with a foaming pint, between them a packet of chilli-flavoured nachos and a salsa dip, he glanced down at his attire. To his horror he saw brown fungal spots – his fig leaf was suffering from rapid fig leaf rot. His wherewithal would soon be without.

At this stage of my tale of love, life, longing and lust (perm as required) I shall spare the blushes and embarrassment of my readers and recount no more, suffice to say there was (and still is) a lot of begatting.

Those of you who wish further details should consult Genesis, chapters 2, 3 and 4.

9 August 2021

A Selection of Short, Sometimes Very Short, Stories

There's An Awful Lot Of It In Brazil

The Headquarters. Room number one. The Chief Executive's office. Peter hesitated. The Boss was a very, very busy man. He always had been, since time began, maybe before that, but this matter was serious. He knocked on the door.

'Come in. Hello, Peter. What can I do for you?'

The man looked ageless, but then he was ageless and immaculate too. Smooth grey hair, a carefully knotted blue silk tie, a suit that he must have been poured into. Glinting gold cufflinks. As if to compensate, Peter observed that there was maybe a trace of lined skin running from the corners of the eyes. Time, time is master of us all. Or is it? Philosophical conundrums were best left for St Augustine, though Peter had heard that some of the Greeks were up and coming in this field.

'Well, governor.'

The CE winced. He had tried for years to wean Peter from his subservient and, he supposed, common manner. And oh for some decent clothes – homespun wool was fine and ethnic … One of his failures, but he never gave up hope, though perhaps it was time to think about a retirement package for this retainer. A small place in a warm clime with good fishing … Peter interrupted.

'It's like this governor. We've just heard that the EC, which stands for …'

'Yes, I know Peter. Go on.'

Vaguely Biblical?

'The EC are discussing a new constitution. No mention of your name. A declaration, like the American one, and this is such a serious matter that I think we should be represented or else they'll make a terrible hash of things.'

The CE nodded. He was becoming more and more disillusioned with his people. He had given them free will but never imagined they would use it so ineptly. It could be a case of back to the drawing board. He would sort that out later. To return to the immediate situation; they would probably get it wrong, but it might be fun to try to influence the resulting words. He rested his chin on his hands and glanced at his family photograph, as though it might provide inspiration.

'It would be no good sending Luke,' he said. 'He would try to reform the health programme and, as we know, Peter, that is technically chaotic and so basically unreformable.'

Peter agreed. The safest thing to do. He didn't understand about chaos, only the primeval kind, and he didn't really understand that.

'And,' the voice continued, 'James would be too bolshie and upset everyone, John is the abstract sort, he would confuse them all with symbols and hidden meanings. Even I can't work out what he is trying to say sometimes. Matthew and Mark can write a good line, but they are unimaginative. Paul would be full of Greek philosophy and want to convert everyone. I guess I had better go myself.'

Peter breathed more easily. It was his duty to keep the Boss one step ahead of the opposition, but he hated trips outside his own secure world. He always felt clumsy and out of place with bureaucrats and politicians.

'That's decided', the CE said. 'How about a coffee.'

Peter shook his head. 'No thanks.'

'Very wise. I don't know why I keep drinking it, it's not very good.'

Peter nodded, said he had a lot of new entrants clamouring at the gates waiting to be vetted, and excused himself.

The CE touched the computer screen on his desk. He really preferred the telephone, but one had to keep up with the technology and the last Chinese delegation had been very persuasive.

'Hello, Mary.' He smiled to himself. Now the family had grown up she said she wanted a job and a bit of independence and with his secretary on maternity leave … 'Book me on a flight to Brussels, please, and arrange some decent accommodation and a hire car. I'm showing the flag so it's five stars and a BMW or a Mercedes.'

He arrived at the massive and sprawling Euro-hive on the outskirts of Brussels, where the fate of the world was decided, at least for a short while. Alas these people had no sense of the scale of time or the flow of history. He easily negotiated armed gatekeepers and electronic countermeasures, and miraculously found a parking slot. He smiled. He would have expected no less.

Such an important meeting naturally attracted all heads of state, democrats to a man, or in one or two cases a woman, some of whom may actually have been elected. Each one was surrounded by advisors, with golden tongues and sharp brains, who could convince you that if you had no bread, a piece of cake would be forthcoming. He selected a seat fortuitously

Vaguely Biblical?

left vacant by the Swiss delegate, with observer status but not voting rights, and smiled at the representatives on either side.

He followed preamble, thrust and counterthrust and lobbed in the occasional question himself. There was so much noise and confusion that no one appeared to notice that he was an observer. The Tower of Babel was still going strong, he was pleased to see.

Momentarily bored, he leaned towards a fellow sufferer on his right. 'Scientists go deeper and deeper into nature and uncover more and more layers of complexity, yet when it comes to human behaviour en masse there is more confusion than ever.'

The Estonian, whose only interest was to reverse one thousand years of history and keep the Russians OUT, agreed.

'And when do we get a coffee break?' the CE added.

On cue, a young intern appeared with refreshments. She no doubt had an excellent understanding of political processes and could advise the President of Liechtenstein on the course to take on high gearing loans if the Swiss franc was devalued against the euro. She was not, however, a waitress. Two coffee cups and a plate of biscuits balanced precariously in her hands and then wobbled before a shower of jammy dodgers descended on the head of the German delegate while hot drinks narrowly missed the British groin. Indignation mixed with the stiff upper lip, and feminine tears flowed.

The CE jumped up, made placatory remarks and put an arm around the girl's shoulders. Immediately everyone stiffened. Sexual harassment. The lawyers would be sharpening their bank balances. He ignored them all.

'What's your name?' he asked.

'Martha' she replied.

'Leave this to me, Martha. You go back and wipe away those tears.'

She disappeared and enlightenment progressed. Until after an hour or so of honest debate and compromise they had a statement of memorable mediocrity which offended no one and meant nothing.

'And to think I could have been out on the golf course,' he said to an Italian.

They agreed on the burdens of leadership and went their ways.

The dark flowing hair in the car park was familiar – Martha.

'How about a lift?' the CE called out.

She looked round. You had to be careful, but the man who had hailed her had been at the meeting and was charming and courteous.

'Thanks. The buses are hopeless at this time and most uncomfortable.'

The blue Mercedes sliced through the traffic and glided to her flat.

'Would you like to come in for a drink,' she asked.

The CE shook his head.

'At least let me give you a packet of Columbian Highland medium roast,' she said. 'It won't take me a minute to get it and I heard that you really liked it earlier today.'

It was Sunday, six days' work completed, the day of rest. He had read the sports pages and noted that his team had managed a draw despite the best efforts of the referee. He should relax but there were a couple of details he needed to check out for Monday morning, even though the world was up and running. He stood in his office looking out over the firmament, his firmament as he liked to remind visiting astronomers, and he saw that it was good.

Mary appeared. Always there when you needed her. 'I've brought you a coffee. Some of that brew that Martha gave you in Brussels.' She spoke the other woman's name with distaste.

'It really has a marvellous flavour, Mary. Why didn't I know about it before? After all, I am supposed to be omniscient …'

She missed the other omni words and turned away muttering. 'Men.'

2 February 2017

Dialogue and Word Play

Dialogue and Word Play

What Is Life For?

Man on top of Clapham Omnibus: so that I can get a better view over Clapham Common.

Charles Darwin: so that it can evolve, and I can study it.

Politician (any): so that it can vote for me and my progressive political agenda that will solve the country's problems.

Chancellor: so that I can tax it.

Viruses, microbes, and bacteria: so that we can have a home.

Donald Trump: never mind the meaning, it was stolen from me by a flawed voting system.

Elon Musk: Twitter, of course.

AI: you only think it exists, actually it is a simulation that can be stopped at any time.

The Chicken: to cross the road.

Judge: it is for the jury to decide, guided by my learned friends in court.

The King: One does wonder at times, but Camilla assures me that one of my sons will explain.

The earth: it's a pity it does, because those eight billion quarrelsome, petulant, people mess everything up.

Zen monk: maybe.

A Selection of Short, Sometimes Very Short, Stories

Walton Street Writers: so that we can write stories.

God: I wonder myself at times.

Oxford philosophy don: I could possibly answer the question in less than one thousand pages of closely reasoned logic; the answer would, however, only be tentative.

Einstein: it's all relative.

Werner Heisenberg: I'm uncertain.

Karl Marx: so that through dialectical argument the proletariat can triumph.

Groucho Marx: who the hell is that guy Karl?

Microsoft Corporation: we're working on it, answer tomorrow when we launch Windows 11. 1.

Hippy: Yeah, like, I knew when I had my last shot of mescaline, now I've forgotten. Need another fix.

Man in pub: damned if I know but make mine a pint.

Neil Hancox: not sure, really.

24 November 2022

Dialogue and Word Play

Assorted Brief (If Inaccurate) Reviews

Treasure Island: a gem.

War and Peace: sadly what happens all the time, somewhere.

The Odyssey: Bill Oddy's sailing home.

The Iliad: what ailed the Greeks and Trojans.

Paradise Lost: Boris goes – you can substitute your own choice of name here.

Paradise Regained: Boris comes back: as above.

A Winter's Tale: what will happen in Britain come November.

Bleak House: ditto.

Great Expectations: a lot of phlegm.

The Old Curiosity Shop: the High Street when Amazon takes over.

A Midsummer Night's Dream: psychedelic hangover after a heavy night.

Hamlet: I can't decide.

The Merry Wives of Windsor: an exposé of royal consorts.

King Lear: that's daughters for you.

Loves Labours Lost: her engagement ring fell down the drain.

A Selection of Short, Sometimes Very Short, Stories

Taming of the Shrew: nature red in tooth and claw.

Arabian Nights: b***** hot.

The Wind in the Willows: cut down on the beans.

Alice in Wonderland: a lot truer than you think.

Anything by Agatha Christie: a mystery to me.

Ulysses: a life sentence.

Crime and Punishment: you commit the crime and reading *Ulysses* is your sentence.

Any book about History: it happened in the past and is examined in great detail.

Das Kapital: Dad's nest egg.

Swann's Way: not too hot on ornithology.

Tales from an Oxford Café: what you hear if you listen in to other people's conversations.

Tales from a Bookshop: as above but more intellectual conversations.

Double Decker: an anthology by the Walton Street Writers: a very large burger.

The Lord of the Flies: zip it up, lad.

Sin and Syntax: yes, it is a book; you commit the first and pay for it.

The Lady of Shallot: knows her onions.

One Hundred Years of Solitude: the missus and I had a row.

The Origin of Species: defeats me but I know there's something odd in my ancestry.

Rupert Bear: no wonder he's shivering.

8 August 2022

A Selection of Short, Sometimes Very Short, Stories

A Conversation for Two

Scene: A secluded but comfortable lounge. A group of smartly dressed men and women standing, chatting, drinking champagne and tucking into canapés.

A. Well it's all over for you and your lot, my turn now.

B. That's right. You'll be off to Buck Pal tomorrow, I imagine.

A. Yes, and then I must select the cabinet.

B. Difficult job, I know. Had to give my Foreign Secretary a world atlas.

A. Mix up Moscow and Manchester? Could be a bit dodgy.

B. And none of my lot had GCSE maths, made it difficult to find a chancellor.

A. Treasury is full of mandarins.

B. But they are either citrus fruit or Chinese.

A. I have my opening speech ready for the House.

B. What will you say? Forward, to the bright future, no more mistakes, hard toil but we will make it.

A. Something like that. Then I say what a mess you left for us. Usual stuff.

B. I know. My lot say the just the same.

A. Of course. It's in the unofficial rule book.

B. Then I reply. Slag you off and wish you luck, you'll need it leading that rabble.

A. That's our fate, but we'll still be able to meet up for a quiet drink, though you might have to smuggle in your own bottle.

B. Swap anecdotes, give advice.

A. Any advice how to keep the proles happy?

B. Bread and circuses.

A. Is that Roman…?

B. Polanski. No, Cicero or some such, I think

A. Well, you should know. Read classics, didn't you?

B. Yes, but I never paid much attention.

A. And what will you do, apart from parliamentary appearances and walking the dog?

B. Had a great idea. Secret meeting with the BBC boss, can't remember his name. Said to him if I should find myself in need, how about an appearance on Strictly, with a gorgeous professional straight from the steppes.

A. Snow on her leotard, eh, to cool your ardour?

B. That's it. Quid pro quo, BBC keep the licence fee.

A. Is the lovely lady, Valentina Arakanova?

B. Yes, that's it.

A. Bad luck, you'll find she's straight from Essex.

2 February 2022

A Selection of Short, Sometimes Very Short, Stories

Opera Café

Car kaput, catastrophic cacophony of coughing, creep into comfortable caff for coffee.

Chrissie at counter, 'Caramel coff or chocolate, with carrots, chorizo, chips, cheesecake, cherries?'

'Columbian, carissima.'

Cup comes, complete with check, on chintz, correct.

'Cheers.'

Cool contents. Choke, cough. Chrissie's cruising, concerned.

Comments, 'Careful.'

Cloakroom.

Counter, coins.

'Do you sing opera?'

'Croon, Cavalleria Rusticana.'

Consternation, cos Mascagni commences with 'm'.

'Chopin?'

'Cheerio, ciao.'

Carefree, cerulean clouds, ciggie, cough, curse.
Caff, Chrissie.
This time, Thai tea.
'Tart, toast, tortilla – tangerine?'
'Ta.'
Tasty. 'Thanks.'
Tenner to Thomas.
'Do you sing opera?'
'Tenor?'
'Traviata?'
'Tchaikovsky.'

Tremble, Terrible.
Toes twitching.
Tarmac, trudge towards town.

2017

A Selection of Short, Sometimes Very Short, Stories

CCP Not PPE

A university admissions tutor is interviewing a student applicant.

T. So you want to study PPE; we don't offer that anymore. We've replaced it with CCP, Cakes, Creative Writing and Politics. Do you understand the common theme?

S. Yes, cakes are made from assorted ingredients, mixed up and baked.

T. Go on.

S. Creative writing is a mix of characters and their stories.

T. And politics?

S. That's ideas and people mixed with hot air, and it usually comes out half baked.

T. You appear to be getting the hang of things. How about some illustrations?

S. Victoria sponge; British through and through, no foreign nonsense. Old fashioned, dependable, bit like Nigel.

T. And a fruit cake?

S. Easy; that's Jeremy.

T. Anything from north of the border?

S. Black bun, solid, ponderous, deep fried and not to be eaten on the Sabbath.

T. Good.

S. There's the squeezed middle; a long doughnut filled with cream; you compress the centre, lick up the cream and throw the rest away. If you don't do that you get terrible indigestion.

T. Sounds like Mills and Boon.

S. How about lemon drizzle cake? Sweet, beguiling, goes bad if left too long in the tin. Bit like a government front bench or one of those best sellers that show great promise until you get halfway through, when you give up.

T. Donna Tart comes to mind, that is if you'll stretch cakes to tarts.

S. Any time, I am particularly fond of the Bakewell variety.

T. What about thrillers?

S. The ultimate comfort food. You suspend belief and live in a world of make believe where all problems are eventually resolved.

T. That sums up economics as well as politics.

S. There's one more; Euro cake. Twenty-seven ingredients, none of which mix, it costs the earth and only the British stick to the recipe.

T. You are an extremely cynical young man with an excellent knowledge of cakes, if nothing else, an ideal candidate for our course. If you used the slogan 'Vote for me and have your cake and eat it', you would be PM in no time. And don't worry about the course fees; you are eligible for the Mr Kipling scholarship.

27 October 2015

A Selection of Short, Sometimes Very Short, Stories

Who's Coming To Dinner?

'Matricide, patricide …'

'Insecticide.'

I looked at Helen. 'Are you taking the piss?'

She tweaked to charm level two. 'Of course not, darling.'

I needed nicotine and alcohol.

However, the doctor's instructions were clear. He put aside his stethoscope.

'It's a dickey ticker, I guess.'

He mouthed a few incomprehensible words.

'Do you want to be resuscitated?' he said.

'What, right now?'

He was twitching and fingering his keyboard.

'Ah, I get it. That's when I'm deleted from the cloud.'

'You are daydreaming,' Helen said.

I slipped back to the present now. She was reclining on the sofa, one shaved and tanned leg crossed over the other.

'You look like the Rokeby Venus,' I told her.

She took a sip of her coffee. 'I recall that she was naked and with her back to the viewer to preserve her modesty.'

'Whereas you are fully clothed and facing me.'

I sighed. 'One-nil in the game of life, though I have forgotten which set.'

'What's this business about the 'cides?' she inquired.

'It's a writing exercise,' I replied, 'comparing the classic stories of Greek literature with the basic plots of today's soaps and serials.'

Helen nodded and moved on to topic two. 'Have you forgotten who is coming to dinner tonight?'

I pretended to search my mind, what remained of it, and came up with the required answer. 'Your mother.'

'So,' Helen rose to charm level three, 'is it to be matricide, or your pleasant side? You decide.'

22 August 2014

Art Stories

Art Stories

Dinner For Two

On this occasion he would use his best writing paper, the thicker sort with the cream finish and a watermark. It was always tempting to use the thinner paper behind which you could insert a lined former to guide your words, as this made for neatness. No, this was too important a letter; the individual touch was required.

A common Biro would not do for the writing. Ballpoint pens flatten the personality, and he must try to get his to shine through. It would be his fountain pen, the one with the gold cap, albeit nine carat and plated, the iridium tipped nib, and royal blue ink. Memo, buy another bottle of ink.

What should he say? His words must be simple, from the heart, not gushing and definitely not pleading. Perhaps, 'Dear Helena, I have read so much about you and admire your paintings and that marvellous self-portrait. I would love you to join me for dinner when we could explore art together.'

That would do for now. But what was her address? Helena in Kent would be most unlikely to find her. Maybe he should send his letter to the publishers of the biography in which she was mentioned so often, and in such detail, and request them to forward it.

The address on the letter he received some weeks later was handwritten, neat precise writing. It wasn't a bill, invoice, circular, surely not a request for money – the end is in sight, one more push, for which we urgently require funds, and the problem is solved. No, none of these.

He opened the envelope carefully using a kitchen knife, more familiar with chopping vegetables than cutting paper, and pulled out the letter.

'Dear Edward,' he read. 'Sadly, my aunt Helena died a while ago. I am her niece, Emily, also an artist. I would be pleased to meet you for dinner.'

There were more details which he ignored in the excitement of receiving a reply. Memo, another shirt and tie, nothing too garish, possibly a new toothbrush.

The next morning, he selected the collective biography of British artists and designers in the mid to late twentieth century from his shelves and reread the section on Helena. A sister was mentioned but there were no other details.

He waited a few days and then replied, accepting her suggested time and place.

The special day arrived. His thinning grey hair had been trimmed, he shaved carefully, rejected his old interview suit, instead dressing smart casual. He polished his shoes; so often a good appearance was betrayed by poorly presented footwear.

The restaurant chosen by Helena's niece, he must remember to call her Emily, was in an area south of the river, which was not yet gentrified but genteel, as though deciding which way to go.

A woman was sitting alone at a table close to the window. She smiled and waved to him.

'Hello, 'she said, 'I'm Emily, you must be Edward.' The introduction was sealed with a handshake.

Emily, he judged, was probably in her early fifties, tall, her face completed with rimless glasses and a wide smile, the hair streaked with grey, pulled back from the forehead. He was not expert in fashion, but her floral dress appeared elegant, expensive.

Over dinner, accompanied by a passable dry white, Emily showed him several of her sketch books. Watercolour was carefully applied over a pencil drawing. The subjects were mostly scenes from rural Kent and Sussex, decaying buildings, old farm machinery. All were rendered in hues of pale browns and greens, restful and recalling quieter, more relaxed times. 'Of course, Edward,' she explained, 'I work these up later into complete pictures, but those are too big and heavy to bring along tonight.'

Reluctantly he produced some examples of his own work, impressionistic acrylic sketches, imprecise by comparison with Emily's detailed work.

He rejected Emily's offer to split the bill. They chatted idly while waiting for a taxi to take her to the railway station and as they parted, she placed a brief kiss on his cheek.

Two bus journeys later and he was back in his flat. It had been an exciting yet relaxed evening. Emily had been polite, even enthusiastic, about his pictures and sketches, though he knew they were nothing compared with her work.

Had he expected a romance? With Helena, maybe. He should have paid more attention to arithmetic at school. Then some simple sums would have shown the discrepancies between the ages of Helena and himself.

He shrugged and poured a nightcap. He decided that there would be no more of these special letters. Memo, bottle of ink, royal blue, to the charity shop. The toothbrush was another matter. His dentist had recently complimented him on the improved condition of both teeth and gums.

Edward awoke next morning with a headache, too generous a nightcap probably, and a nagging question: should he send a note to Emily? The issue was resolved a day or so later when a letter arrived for him addressed in that neat and precise handwriting he now associated with his new friend. She thanked him for a delightful evening and invited him to a private viewing of her next exhibition in London, a couple of months hence.

The gallery, dowdy from the outside he thought at first but welcoming indoors, was busy, smart people drinking wine and talking loudly. He wanted to leave, slip away, but Emily spotted him, detached herself from a chattering group and introduced him to a young man who called her Mum. Slowly the single word sank into Edward's consciousness. He was bemused, shell shocked. Why had he never anticipated that Emily might have a family? He had noticed no wedding ring when they had met for dinner. He wiped a trace of moisture from his brow.

'It's the sudden heat inside,' he said. 'I'll be fine in a minute.'

Emily's son swept up two glasses of white wine from a passing tray, gave one to Edward, and began to steer the older man around the paintings, explaining the background and pointing out details that would have easily passed unnoticed by Edward.

There was one special picture, no more than forty inches wide by thirty tall, in a broad beech wood frame, a view of gently rolling downs, fields and fences, seen from a railway carriage, third class. Edward knew immediately that he must buy it, whatever the cost, for it would complete his relationship with Emily and art.

Back in his flat he cleared a wall and selected the ideal space for the new picture.

Art Stories

This wonderful image would comfort him for ever, in sickness and health…

29 December 2021

O & E

The two men were sitting at a scrubbed café table. Beside either man were some playing cards, a few sous, a glass of absinthe and a heap of sugar cubes.

Close by, a young couple were holding hands.

'She has the pallor of death etched into her skin,' the older man said.

The other nodded. 'Her lover will be devastated when she dies. I wonder if he will travel to Hades to retrieve her, like Orpheus?'

'Tell me that story,' his friend said. 'I know you have the learning.'

The younger man was secretly pleased that his knowledge, acquired despite the old school master who beat them all, was requested. He paused. 'When Eurydice died in childbirth,' he began, 'her lover Orpheus was so overcome that he went down to Hades to plead with the Queen of the Night for the return of his beloved. He took his lyre and sang so beautifully that the Queen shed tears that turned to diamonds as they fell and eventually agreed that he could take Eurydice back to life. But on one condition.'

'There always is,' the other man said.

'The condition was,' his friend continued, 'that he must not look back until Hades was behind them, On the very last step Orpheus' longing for his lover was so overwhelming that he glanced over his shoulder and Eurydice disappeared forever. He was distraught and walked away sobbing. A group of young men about town laughed at him and kicked him to death.'

Art Stories

The speaker's companion placed a sugar cube between his lips and sucked at the bitter absinthe. 'That's so sad,' he said. And then added, 'Another hand?'

The other man stared into space as he picked up his cards. 'You know the story of the red diamonds, do you? As the women lifted up the body of Orpheus, hundreds of small red diamonds fell onto the shroud. They collected them, pasted them onto sheets of parchment, and today we play games of chance with the tears of the Queen of the Underworld.'

The older man smiled. 'You owe me four sous.'

A slim waisted, tall woman, with black hair piled on top of her head, placed both her hands on their table. 'I heard you speaking about Orpheus and Eurydice,' she said. 'You should go to the theatre and see Mr Offenbach's new opera about them. The songs are wonderful, and it will only cost you a few francs.'

As the two men stared at the white flesh flowing downwards from her throat, she disappeared.

'Time to go,' they both agreed. 'We have to be at the iron foundry at 6.00 a.m. tomorrow.

'Maybe one day we will have a few francs,' one of them said.

His friend laughed. 'By then we will both be deaf.'

Undated

A Selection of Short, Sometimes Very Short, Stories

The Painted Lady

'Ouch.'

Robert sucked at the spot of blood on the tip of his finger and cursed people who use staples instead of paper clips. A passing colleague queried the red colour.

'Thought yours would have been blue.'

He glared at the girl. The way she moved reminded him of Sally and that depressed him. He needed cheering up. Why not call in at lunch time at the new gallery close by?

Just past one o'clock, Robert was standing in front of a painting by Vuillard. The words of the caption, too small to be read without peering, stated that this was an early twentieth century work entitled 'A Woman Sewing'. The woman appeared to be in her mid to late forties. She had auburn hair and her left shoulder was turned towards the viewer. The walls of the room were covered with heavy drapes, while the gas light in the corner, Robert thought, must have been inadequate for delicate needlework. The result would surely have been eye strain.

'Hello?' Soft and questioning. 'Hello.' Rather more insistent this time. 'Are you going to ignore me? I get very lonely sitting here, forever completing the same piece of embroidery.'

'I'm sorry to hear that.' Robert heard his own words and swallowed. It must have been an automatic response. Pull yourself together, man. He was young and sane, not yet given to muttering to himself in public. He tried to move on, but his feet failed to respond. The woman was immobile with her needle poised above the cloth, as it had been for a hundred years. Robert wiped a thin film of sweat from his forehead. Work had been stressful lately – awkward clients. He'd been skipping lunch and drinking too much in the evening. Perhaps he should take advantage of the health check-up the company was offering.

'My name's Soligne. I'm French.'

'And I'm Robert, and I don't talk to women whose faces I can't see and who are made of paint.'

'Doesn't your wife use powder and rouge? Maybe you have a mistress?' There was a gentle laugh and two dark eyes looked out at him. Eyes, travelling slowly towards middle age, tinged with the first lines of sadness at the corners. 'Now you can see my face.'

The voice continued. 'I'm set in time. It's immortality I suppose. I shall never get any older. Many people might envy me. They forget that I'll never see my grandchildren. Enough! You could come to visit me for half an hour. No one would be jealous. How could they be? Let's say four o'clock tomorrow afternoon.'

The head was lowered, and Robert was staring at an oil painting in an art gallery a few hundred yards from his office. If he wasn't mistaken, the brushwork was a little hurried in the left-hand corner. Perhaps the artist had become bored with the model? Robert could understand that. He had been suffering from similar ill-defined feelings lately. The musing was disturbed by a brusque, 'Excuse me,' as an attendant steered him out of the way to allow a mother and an unwilling child in a pushchair to pass.

'What's the matter with him?' Speculation on Robert's state of mind and, even for one so lithe and active, his physical health, reverberated around the office from screen to screen, courtesy of email.

'Susie's dumped him.'

'Rubbish, he's been with Sally for years. She's trying to hook him.'

'Are you sure?'

'He's probably getting restless.'

At home that evening, the interest continued.

'You are not paying attention, Robert. Has it been very stressful today?' The words were accompanied with a frown and half a smile.

He could answer truthfully. 'Yes, darling.'

And there it rested while he diverted himself with indifferent television images. He was in one of his enigmatic moods, Sally knew. Better leave it to evaporate.

The next morning, he passed breakfast behind his paper, was alternately short tempered and indulgent with clients and breathless with indecision. He had only popped into the gallery on a whim and now he was dating a virtual woman, when he had the real thing in his bed.

That afternoon he found an excuse for leaving work early. The gallery closed at five o'clock. That would give him an hour with Soligne. On the way he stopped to buy roses from a street seller. The woman sensed his agitation. 'Forgotten her birthday, duckie, or is it someone new?'

He ignored the proffered change, and the woman turned her charms on the next punter.

There she was, his faithful seamstress. Faithful. He had only met her yesterday. What was happening to him?

'Come in.'

Art Stories

'How?'

'Most of my visitors use the door.'

He sensed the edge of sarcasm. The room was cosy, too dark for his taste. Victorian, Robert thought, but that was reasonable for around 1900, even if it was supposed to be France.

'Hello, I'm Soligne. But you knew that.' She remained in her seat and extended a hand. Mottling was beginning to establish itself on the skin.

'And I'm Robert.' He proffered the roses.

'Thank you. They are so beautiful. Such a deep red. It is a long time since a man bought me flowers.' She rang a bell on the table beside her and a maid glided in, gathered up the bouquet and disappeared. Ten minutes later the roses reappeared in a cut-glass vase, followed by a silver tray with two cups, an elegant coffee pot, a bowl of sugar and some small cakes.

'A little black coffee to wash away the weariness of the afternoon. A cake to fortify you before your supper. If you are like my husband, you never have time to eat properly before your dinner.'

Robert nodded. He sat on a chair that was more uncomfortable than it looked. Soligne smiled, removed a skein of silk and several needles and patted the sofa.

'Come and sit here, Robert. That chair is an antique. For show only. My husband thinks it is elegant.' She shrugged.

Robert was mesmerised by the yellow light flecking her hair and the feminine scent. Violets, lilies? He gave up. Soligne chattered away. The apartment had two bedrooms, a salon where they were now and a dining room. She entertained her husband's business friends there. The neighbours were quiet, retired. The streets were noisy though with people always in a hurry and horse drawn carriages and carts. That was why she kept the windows closed.

'Do you spend a lot of time sewing?' Robert asked.

She shook her head.

'You sew buttons on shirts, you sew up holes in stockings. This is embroidery. Your wife will know the difference, Robert.'

He doubted it. Sally never mended anything. If it needed fixing, throw it out, was her motto. He caught himself. What was he doing here? He had left work early; he had bought flowers and all for a woman he had only just met and …

'You look distracted, Robert. Tell me about yourself, your family, what you do. Maybe you are a gentleman of leisure?'

Poor boy, he was scarcely into manhood, but she would humour him. He seemed hypnotised. That was a popular word in the theatre at the moment.

How do you tell a woman bathed by gaslight, whose husband probably takes a carriage to work, that you interact with a computer, hold video conferences with Australia and China, and fly to America several times a year? He hesitated and wondered if he should explain that he wasn't married. His thoughts were jumbled and so were his words. Soligne picked up a needle and started to thread it with purple silk. This man was becoming a disappointment. He was like so many younger males, uninteresting, unimaginative.

Robert looked at his watch, aware of the anachronism of digital quartz, and brushed her hand with a kiss.

'I must go now. Get back to my work.'

A dismissive smile.

'Goodbye.'

Robert needed time to think. He walked the last mile or so to his home trying to sort out chaotic emotions. Perhaps his heart would be more useful than his brain? He loved Sally, or did he? They had a joint mortgage and holidayed in the Maldives. She was very sexy. Was he suffering relationship fatigue? He liked that term. Oh God, what was he doing lured by this siren?

'Hi, darling.' The words seemed to part the blond hair that had fallen over her face. 'You're late. Working hard, I expect.'

He didn't contradict.

'I'm glad it's Friday,' he said, 'and we can relax together. We could ask your sister over tomorrow. You know how she likes to show off the baby. Go to a film. Dinner out.' His inventiveness seemed endless and just a little alarming.

Sally nodded. 'Ummm, tell you in the morning.'

Another breakfast, another bedful of crumbs, the paper liberally spread around. Uncombed hair. Laziness.

'I've decided.' It was Sally's firm voice. 'I want to be cultured. After lunch we'll go to that new art gallery.'

Robert managed a strangulated 'Yes' and remembered ninety-nine jobs that required immediate attention.

'Been in here before, Robert?'

'In passing, as they say. Saw it was new and thought I'd pop my head around the door.'

She stopped in front of the Vuillard.

'Good, isn't it?'

'Bit dark for me,' he said automatically.

Something made him look again. The deep red bouquet, placed on a side table, grinned at him. He turned his head away hurriedly. Was she talking to the woman?

Sally tugged at his arm and pointed. 'Look, darling, at those red roses. You never buy me red roses.'

19 January 2006

Art Stories

Pigment

The first stone kicked up a spurt of dust at the feet of the sleeping man. The second hit his left leg just below the knee. Pietro shook his head, wiped the dribble from his chin, rubbed his leg and tried to focus his freshly opened eyes. He saw the two urchins crouching a few feet away. As he swore and reached for his staff the boys took to their heels.

'What is the world coming to?' he shouted.

An old woman, shuffling by, nodded.

The water trough was pushing into his back, his feet were sore, and his head ached. The flea bites, picked up the night before in the yard of the inn, itched. The package was safe in the left-hand pocket of his breeches and his money and food were untouched. The cold water gurgling behind him sounded inviting. He rolled over into a kneeling position and splashed his eyes and face, rinsed out his mouth and spat into the dust at his feet. Time for some food. The torn square of cloth held the last of the hard cheese, a piece of harder bread and a few dried figs. A tongue lazily explored the back teeth. Another one was loose. Better soak the bread in water. The food finished, Pietro wiped his mouth with the sleeve of his jerkin and completed his toilette by running his fingers through his thick brown curls. Although it was at least twenty-three years since his birth his hair still brought catcalls and comments from unwary strangers.

It couldn't be far now. The young girl looked puzzled at his request for directions, shrugged and ran away. The man was different. Despite his scarred and tanned face, he was happy to talk to the stranger and tell him how to get to the artist's house. Thirty or forty minutes' walk through the centre of the town, branch right up the hill and it was the building with the imposing tower studded with windows. Pietro thanked him and made his way through the increasingly busy streets and tiny squares. The scents of spices and foodstuffs drifting from the small shops were mixed with those of animal and human sweat and much worse in places. The market stalls, with their displays of fruit and vegetables, meat and fish, trinkets and cloth, were centres of noise. Some of the young girls were coquettish and pursued by groups of swaggering young men, pushing aside anyone unwise enough to step into their path. Dirty children darted underfoot but mainly, as everywhere, the people seemed old, worn and stained by life. Nothing new here, Pietro, thought. It was similar forty miles to the south where he lived.

The house with the tower. He could see the windows in two of the sides and guessed there would be matching ones in the other two walls – artists need light. The main courtyard was open to the road. As he strode in, he was greeted by two dogs. The leading one snapped at his feet and made to jump at him. The staff came up effortlessly and caught the dog in the ribs, hard enough to knock it back but not do any real damage. The path was clear to the small, shaded room at the far end. Here the guardian was an ill-tempered middle-aged woman with pointed black eyes.

'What do you want?' she snapped.

'I have come to see the master. Signor da Vinci.'

'Bah.' She laughed displaying two brown teeth at either side of her lower jaw.

'Away with you, peasant.'

Pietro pulled himself up to his full height, towering above the woman.

'I have come two days' journey to bring the master a new pigment, an unearthly aethereal blue.'

His words were beginning to flow but she cut short the speech.

'The master has bishops and princes, princesses, scheming rulers, wealthy merchants and Popes come to visit him and waste his time. He sends them all away. You, we set the dogs on you. Be off.'

She seemed exhausted by this sudden outburst and disappeared down a dark narrow passage into the interior of the house leaving the caller alone in the room.

Pietro was tired and disappointed, though not surprised. Nobody liked travelling salesmen. He had walked for two days. What could he do? Walk back and tell his beloved Donatella that he had again been unsuccessful. No, he would make the great man listen. The heavy oak door must lead to the tower. He tried it. It was unlocked, the wooden stairs inviting. He climbed confidently but with a shortness of breath and rapid heartbeat that had nothing to do with exertion. The stairs emptied into a large barn-like room with canvasses stacked around the walls, shelves covered with pots, containers, pestles and mortars, pigments, brushes and secret, sweet smelling solutions. A large easel in the centre of the room stood with a board already primed and waiting. Behind and to one side was a couch covered with a thick green velvet cloth awaiting some nubile young woman to model for the

Virgin Mary. He had seen it all many times before. It was reassuringly similar, though if he was honest, disappointing. He had imagined that the studio of so great an artist would be somehow different.

As he turned round one last time, he noticed it. The completed painting, ready to frame. A few hands breadths in size. A woman's head, full face. Dark flowing hair, quizzical eyes. The shoulders covered decorously with a thin wrap of silk. A mistress, perhaps the great man's mistress. She would be one of many, Pietro guessed. Whoever she was, she was stunning apart from one detail. Why was there no smile? The mouth tuned down at the corners and gave her, if not a sullen look, at least one of disinterest. Pietro's legs seemed to work independently of his mind. They carried him over to a palette with some small patches of paint on it and even a fine brush nearby. He mixed up a scraping of the right colour, experimented with it on the back of his own hand and very carefully altered the corners of the mouth, to give just a hint of a smile, an enigmatic smile. The palette was returned, and the brush cleaned.

Now he was sweating and trembling at his boldness and engulfed in waves of a euphoric happiness that he had never known existed. He had at last served his purpose in life and was fulfilled. The picture, he was totally certain, would be famous as long as there were people on the earth, and after that in heaven, and it would have been his hand, his soul that had completed the perfection. He sauntered down the stairs, through the empty anteroom and across the courtyard. He hardly bothered to kick out at the growling curs.

Home now. Donatella would fuss him and feed him, and his tiny daughter would cling to his leg, beg for sweetmeats and then run off to play. His son, it must be a son, swelling in his beloved's belly would kick and push in anticipation of freedom. He laughed out loud, pulled the packet of pigment from his pocket and tossed into a ditch. No need for that anymore. Donatella would pull him into their bed and then suddenly her mood would darken. How were they to feed four mouths and more? What would become of them, where would she get the money for a new dress? The list would be endless but now he had the answer. For three years he had resisted her father's pleas to give up his wandering life and instead get up at four o'clock in the morning to bake bread. The old man had hinted, nay shouted, that Donatella as his only child, would inherit the ovens, the mixing vats, the customers. If she did not, her man could, if her man knew one end of a loaf from another. Now that he, Pietro, had accomplished his life's work he would say yes to the old man and settle into a contented life as a small-town baker. There would be happiness and disappointments too, but he could accept these now.

The coins in his pockets were heavier and his parched throat told him to spend some of them on a jug of strong red wine from the hot plains to ease his homeward journey.

21 September 2002

A Selection of Short, Sometimes Very Short, Stories

The Kiss

'What are you doing, Auguste?' she shouted.

'Thinking.'

'You are always thinking and that doesn't put bread in the mouths of your family. And don't say, "Give them cake."'

Rosa, who was still awaiting the gold ring that would make her Madame, walked further into the studio and saw Auguste hunched up, sitting on a block of marble, no doubt Carrara's finest, with his clenched fist resting on his forehead.

'I expect,' she said, 'that all this mess,' she indicated piles of clay, marble chippings, bits of wire, wood and paper, 'gets you down. You should let me clear it up for you. Or better get one of those young mademoiselles who always seem to be hanging around, without any clothes, to do it. It would help keep them warm.'

His wife, as Auguste thought of her, was such a kind hearted, thoughtful, woman. He pushed himself up off the cold block of stone, brushed the dust from his smock and walked over to her.

'I salute you with my lips,' he said, proffering a kiss.

She noted, mechanically, that this erotic offering tasted of cheap tobacco and unspecified dust with just a hint of garlic.

'Your lunch is ready,' she said.

As they walked together towards the rugged farmhouse kitchen, Auguste remarked, 'I thought you said earlier that there was no bread.'

'I was speaking metaphorically,' she replied. 'It's meat. I sweet talked the butcher into extending my credit.'

He returned to silence, pondering the difficulties of living with an intellectual. When he could snatch a moment from his work he must consult a dictionary, or better still ask that well-bred mademoiselle who had promised to model for him, to explain metaphor.

Lunch completed, the rustic plate wiped clean with a crust of bread, which he thought did not exist, washed down with a glass of vin ordinaire, a dash of cognac and a coffee, he was propelled back towards his studio, with the exhortation, 'Earn some money, complete one of those commissions you are always talking about.'

He contemplated the marble seat again and then remembered his mother's warning that excessive cold applied to the nether regions could result in piles. He did not wish to add to his sea of troubles and decided to stand.

'Monsieur Auguste.' A childlike voice disturbed his thoughts. Angelique smiled, tripped across the floor and kissed him. 'I have come,' she said, 'to be your model.' Artist though he was, familiar with all the ins and out of the female form, he immediately forgot about bodily pains and the meaning of metaphor, as she slipped out of her flimsy dress and pulled him down towards the marble slab. They mutually saluted one another with their lips.

Suddenly he pulled away. He had caught sight of their entwined bodies in a handily placed mirror. 'Stay exactly like that,' he shouted and to reinforce the pose he propped her in place with several pieces of wood, while he sketched furiously.

A Selection of Short, Sometimes Very Short, Stories

'You do not like me, my young, lithe body?' Angelique asked with tears in her eyes.

Auguste put down his charcoal and paper and smiled at her. 'You are perfect, my dear, and one day you will be seen and loved across the globe. Now, however I have work to do.'

The wire armature was shaped, and the clay moulded, night and day, until the sculpting was perfect. Eventually the mould was completed, and the bronze casting emerged, the first of many copies to be seen in museums and parks everywhere. The Kiss was realised.

Madame was broad-minded, helped by a plenteous flow of francs; not so other ladies from the moral elite who believed that such verisimilitude would inflame the passions of the common man. Fortunately for art lovers their fears failed to materialise.

Angelique sought consolation, and ultimately respectability, in the arms of the local draper; the butcher's bill was paid; bread was plentiful; and Auguste never did find out what metaphor meant.

10 May 2002

History or Something!

A Selection of Short, Sometimes Very Short, Stories

A Letter To My Agent

'William.' The voice was unsmiling.

He adjusted his doublet and pushed the manuscript away. Should he choose the ornate reply, 'My dearest what plagues your throat that such an utterance comes forth?' or simply say 'Yes'? Experience suggested the latter.

'Yes, my dear, what is the matter?'

'Have you written to your agent yet enclosing your latest story? The children and I are tired of gruel and desire some meat, and don't even suggest poaching.'

He was undone and placed inked quill upon parchment. Maybe he could appeal to the lack of foreign carters due to Elizabeth's latest spat with the Spanish. No, he had already tried that approach.

The letter was completed and despatched to London Town by a reliable courier.

Surprisingly quickly a reply appeared. 'My dear William,' it began. 'There is little appetite or sales for books due to the lack of education among most of the population. Plays however, depending on the spoken word which even our masses can comprehend, are increasingly popular. Take one of your books and treat it thus. Try for instance, "Dire and dirty dealings amongst the heather, or why the king forever sleeps uneasy in his bed", and change the title to something more memorable, nay snappy, say, "Macbeth".'

This time the quill flew across the parchment, the ink pot was drained and filled again and again, and there was a run on oak gall, until the grand opening at the Globe.

With a reputation hopefully in the bag, our hero filched some pennies from a jar in the kitchen and slipped out to the tap room of 'The Good Queen Bess', colloquially 'Betty's Boozer' for a celebratory tankard of foaming ale. There, in a corner, he espied fellow writers Ben Jonson and Christopher Marlowe and a thin rakish fellow pretending to be one of the common people but not truly succeeding. 'Let me introduce myself, Edward de Vere, Earl of Oxford,' the man said, extending a whitened hand ending in be-ringed fingers. Languid, William thought. He would soon tire of pushing a quill across even the smoothest paper.

The Earl called for wine. As he poured each one of them a glass, he placed an arm across William's shoulders. 'Anne hath a way with her,' he said, winking at the others.

16 October 2021

A Selection of Short, Sometimes Very Short, Stories

William S and Fame

The playwright lounged at his oaken desk. A fireplace to roast his persona in winter's cold and rage, a large window opened to cool his brow in summer, though this didst allow the pestilence and noise of the common people cheap entrance as well. To one side his secretary, to the other his personal scribe ready for dictation, and Juliette, slim, pale, virginal.

There was a commotion downstairs. 'Tis our own Mercury, our winged messenger from Old London Town,' the scribe exclaimed.

A flustered man, with no sign of wings on his stout boots, burst into the chamber and thrust a scroll at William. Juliette unpicked the ribbon and slid a stiletto beneath the waxen seal. She handed the parchment to William.

'Tis from the EU,' he exclaimed, his voice laced with rising alarm. 'Is it European? Hath Hamlet returned to haunt me, Timon of Athens, the Merchant of Venice?'

'Or Two Gentlemen from Verona?' the scribe added.

His secretary, used to such outbursts, coughed. 'No, sire, 'tis from the Elizabethan Entertainment Corporation, a worshipful company registered in London, designed to bring jollification and entertainment to the poor and downtrodden such that they forget their ague, plague and pox, icy hovels and rotting meat.'

William interrupted. 'Careful, sire. Agents of our gracious queen crouch at every keyhole and sidle into dark corners ready to carry messages of treason to her

History or Something

ear. Take care or your head will be at Houndsditch and your bottom at Bethnal Green, and then great hunger will pursue you, whatever viands are offered to your mouth.'

Ignoring this warning, the secretary continued to read. 'They wish, sire, that you take part in Strictly Come Prancing, as a celebrity.'

'Come, prithee tell me what is this Strictly? 'William enquired. Pale Juliette sprang to life again.

''Tis an exhibition of the Terpsichorean arts,' she intoned. 'You and your professional partner entertain the masses with twists and twirls and fancy footwork, accompanied by lute and tabor. When all gyrations are complete, the people vote for their favourite couple.'

'No doubt with brickbats, eggs and rotten tomatoes,' the scribe added.

'And who shall my partner be in this entertainment?' William asked, ignoring the dangers of participation.

'Ah, sire,' his secretary said, ''twill be a voluptuous Russian vision from the Volga.'

'Or a scrubber from the steppes,' Juliette added with catlike charm.

'And will her ... ?'

'Of certainty, my sire, encompassed, supported and sustained, but barely so, by finest silks from Tartary, the life's work of a million worms sacrificed all to glorify her figure and beauty, and dyed in imperial purple.'

'Away with such myriad minutiae.' William seized a willing Juliette around the slimness of her waist and began. 'One, two, three.' He hesitated.

'Four,' the scribe supplied the missing word.

'I know that, thou minion of stupidity, but does the foot go back or forth?'

A draught swept into the chamber followed by a wife, a mother, a mistress, and master of them all.

'Anne,' four voices intoned in unison, if not in tune. William's arm descended to its natural state of repose. The scribe, at heart a simple being without guile or sense, despite his skills with quill and ink, sought to mitigate their state of anxious surprise. 'The master is no satyr,' he observed, 'merely one who demonstrates the skills of foot and timing.'

A sinewy hand seized his ear and propelled him down the wooden staircase with neither care nor gentleness. In the kitchen a pointed shoe of the latest provincial fashion, delivered a mighty blow to the confluence of hose and pantaloon. A silent mouth opened to show gaping red bestrewed with ivory stumps, two bloodshot eyes soared skyward in their sockets and a body sank towards the floor.

A passing kitchen maid, her face obscured by bone-worn, redded hand, muttered, 'That Anne hath such a way with her.'

24 October 2021

History or Something

Adieu, Goodbye, Farewell

Dame Anne – she tasted the recent title with less satisfaction than afore – looked down at the wasting figure lying 'mongst the down and sheets. The rattling breath disturbed the layerings of sweat and puffed the vivid cheeks into momentary life. 'The ague takes its course,' she muttered.

'And Frenchie wines doth augment the evil plague,' a scribe at her shoulder added in thought, if not in voice.

'An apothecary,' she commanded, 'and no snot-nosed sullen apprentice.'

The wizened figure crept into the bedchamber encumbered by pots and potions, leeches and a rusty scalpel. He clutched the silver pennies thrust upon him and selected coloured draughts. In truth he knew that Nature held this soul's fate betwixt her thumb and finger. But he must earn his bread.

'Drink this, sire.' He held a beaker to the quivering mouth and liquid dribbled down throat, chin and chest. The bony frame coughed and heaved; the head lay back.

Dame Anne, now wishing she were plain Anne again, wiped off a tear with lacen cuff.

The stout oaken boards encased the corpse, the cold dark earth received them both. Earls and kings, peasants, dukes, prostitutes and fools crowded round, all creations of the magic quill and febrile mind, scarce knowing their fate now their master had gone.

'Anne hath no more a way with her,' townsfolk cried. She shrank into black drapes and vanished.

10 November 2021

History or Something

The Path

The clear area was several bow shots wide. On either side were trees, not the scrub which had been his companion as he descended into the valley. Towards one edge there was a stream. He quietened his horse. By rights he should have been riding a war horse but this mountain pony, which had cost him the last of his silver, was better on the steep and uneven tracks he was using.

There was no smell of smoke in the thickening air, birds were singing, and a fine haze of insects smothered his face. It had been cold when he left the mountain fort at dawn. He had pulled his coarse woollen shirt and trews close to his body, and added his leather jerkin and helmet covered with iron. Now his body was sweating, the wool irritating his skin. Maybe it was lice, not sweat that was the problem. When the young girl had washed his clothes earlier, he had used his dagger to tease vermin out of the crevices. He could have easily missed a few.

The area seemed safe, and pony and rider needed rest. The stream was fast running, the water cold. When they had quenched their thirst, the pony munched on some tolerable grass while the man filled his helmet and poured water over his head.

He checked his saddle bag. There was rough dark bread, so hard it helped to dip it in the stream before chewing it, cheese and thin strips of dried meat. At the bottom he felt something else, dried berries wrapped in leaves. The young girl, with blonde hair and blue eyes, who had shared his bed and nursed his shoulder with herbal poultices, must have put the fruit in his bag. She had smiled and not demanded silver or gold for everything. What was her name? Gwen? He didn't blame the others, they were frightened, but a smile would have been welcome.

The sun was past midday. It was at least another six hours riding before he touched the northern outpost where he had heard there was still some Romano-British order, and he could expect sanctuary. He remounted, made sure his sword was free in its scabbard and that his round shield could be pulled into place quickly.

The trees faded and the track wound between small hummocky hills covered with brush and gorse. The motion of the pony almost lolled him to sleep. He wiped sweat from his face. It was a glint of light that caught his eye. Immediately wary, his right hand touched the hilt of his sword. Flight was not possible. Voices from either side of the path; eight men appeared in front of him. A Saxon raiding party, opportunistic warriors looking for plunder, slaves or simply bored. The men were a head taller than he was and maybe ten or more years younger.

The first spear crashed into the ground in front of him, not by accident, he knew. The raiders hoped he would surrender so that they could rob and kill or enslave him easily. He dismounted. If his pony was injured, it might fall and trap him. It would be better on foot. The next spear hit his shield. The impact made him stagger and the men rushed at him. He slashed at one, knocking the Saxon to the ground. His sword bit into the chest of his next attacker. He slapped the flank of his pony, sending it skittering off.

In the melee the razor-sharp edge of a spear blade sliced into the side of his neck. As the blood pulsed out, he downed another and another assailant. Off balance again, a blade was driven into his body under his armoured coat. The light was hazy. He saw the girl's face dissolve into nothingness.

'He's dead.' The leader of the raiders pointed at the rider's body. They counted their losses. One dying, three badly wounded, who would pass into the netherworld to join their comrade in one, two days, raving, moaning, begging for water.

They started to strip the body of the horseman. The clothes were worn and blood soaked, not worth keeping. A small piece of silver hung round the neck. One of the Saxons, a man with some letters, traced out 'Art', but could make no more.

'Do we leave the body for the crows?' one asked. The leader shook his head. 'He fought well, a worthy opponent. We'll put the body over there.' He pointed to a lake surrounded by reeds. 'You take the head, I'll take the feet.' There was a splash and the remains disappeared.

Dark clouds were rolling in from the east and the Saxons could hear the voice of Thor coming closer and closer. The rain began to lash at them as streaks of yellow light ripped through the sky. Their leader picked up the victim's sword, examined it – heavier than the Saxon type – and raised it above his head, shaking the weapon at the sky. He screamed, twisted and as he fell to the ground the sword jerked from his hand into the water. The three remaining warriors glanced at the body and fled.

30 May 2020

A Selection of Short, Sometimes Very Short, Stories

The Path Revisited

The clearing was about fifty yards wide. On either side were stunted, uneven, trees, not the bracken that had accompanied Archie and Ginny as they descended into the valley. The air was heavy and sticky. It had been cold when they left the hostel in the hills of North Wales. Now they felt overdressed. Fleeces were removed. As they were about to stuff them into their rucksacks, Ginny noticed the stream. It looked cold, bubbling and inviting.

'What are you doing, Archie?' Ginny shouted as she saw her companion scoop up water. 'There could be a dead sheep back there.' She pointed to the way they had come.

He tossed the water on his face. 'OK. We have been walking for three hours time for a snack. I wonder what's in their packed lunches? They cost enough.'

'Don't complain,' Ginny replied. 'I had to carry yours as well as mine, and you said that the bar prices were very competitive.'

She tossed him a brown paper bag. 'Tuna mayo on brown, a chocolate bar, apple and bag of crisps,' he announced.

'Ditto,' Ginny added, 'except it's cheese and tomato on white for me.'

Archie was not sure if ditto was wholly appropriate here. Despite her slim build and blue eyes, behind overly large glasses, which seemed to cover half her face, Ginny could be argumentative and linguistic niceties might be better left unsaid.

History or Something

After fifteen minutes, Archie stood up. 'Time we were on our way.' He stretched to his full height of six feet, jammed his cap on top of a mop of dark hair, removed a stone, real or imaginary, from one of his boots and was ready. He pointed. 'Luckily we are going downhill.'

Ginny retied her blonde hair into a ponytail and hefted her rucksack on to her back. She looked at her companion. He had an easy manner and a slim taut body. Annoyingly, though, he could be pedantic and make up details if he did not know the answer to one of her questions.

Her thoughts were interrupted by a ragged series of 'Hellos' as a party of eight young men and women, in army fatigues and carrying massive packs, moved past them upwards towards the mountains.

'Rather them than me,' Ginny said to Archie as the pair started to walk. The trees soon disappeared behind them, and they emerged into a landscape of rounded hummocky hills. 'They remind me of gently moulded breasts,' Ginny said. Archie agreed though with such a choice what would … he fantasised.

'How are we doing for time?' Ginny enquired.

Archie sighed. His companion seemed overly anxious. 'The manager of the hostel said it was a six-hour tramp to the main road and that there was a bus to Chester every hour.' He consulted his watch and the map. 'We are over halfway, I reckon another two and half hours and we should make the road just before four o'clock.'

The invisible biting insect life was becoming more worrisome. They stopped to apply the repellent sold at the hostel to exposed body parts. While Ginny was making certain every exposed piece of her flesh was adequately covered, Archie wandered off towards a flat area dotted with reeds. Suddenly he shouted and swore. Ginny ran over to him. 'Careful,' he said, 'the ground's very boggy here and I've already stepped in well over my boots.'

As he extracted his foot, he dragged up a piece of metal. 'It's a sword,' he yelled excitedly. 'Look.' He thrust it towards the girl. It appeared to her to be a strip of rusty metal. Archaeology was going to be Archie's thing at university, Ginny had found out last night, so perhaps he saw things differently.

The young man wrapped up the remains in a tee shirt, tied the package to his walking pole for protection and put it into his rucksack. 'A walking pole was helpful to the knees going downhill but sometimes you had to make a sacrifice,' he explained to Ginny.

The couple hit the main road in time to get the four o'clock bus to Chester and signed into a B & B. Later, over a Chinese meal they talked about their plans. It was a mere 24 hours since they had met at the bar in the hostel and in reality, they knew little about one another, other than that there was a certain animal attraction.

Next morning, after Archie had consumed the full English, both his own and most of Ginny's, they were ready to go. First, however, he insisted they call in at the local museum.

When the circumstances and location of the find had been logged, a reluctant curator was persuaded to see them. As an impatient Archie unwrapped the exhibit it began to disintegrate leaving shards of rust on the cloth.

The young man's shoulders sagged. The curator and Ginny felt his disappointment. 'Sacrificial weapons are sometimes dredged up in the area you mentioned,' the official intoned, 'and this might have been an example. The brackish soil preserves them but once exposed to air they rapidly disintegrate. I'll keep the pieces if that's all right with you,' he added, 'and we will run some tests.'

They parted at the bus station with a hug and a kiss, off to opposite sides of the country before starting university. 'I'll text you,' Archie said, in a half-hearted way. His disappointment was still raw. Ginny nodded. He had been mostly good company, but her mind was already flooding with the prospect of fresh experiences and new friends. At least her walking boots had been properly broken in.

5 June 2020

Based on Nursery Rhymes/Myths

Based on Nursery Rhymes/Myths

Another Cautionary Tale

'What's for dinner?' four voices shouted in unison, while banging knives and forks on the oak table, recently acquired in the sales.

The loudest voice belonged to Ferdinand King, father of the triplets, Mandy, Randy and Bandy, whose vocal cords were in a more formative stage of development. Mandy, who despite her nickname, was very feminine, full of wiles and sadly bullied by the family, sat next to her father. Randy was nearly christened Randolph, but this proved too long a name for this family to remember. Bandy, whose legs were as straight as beanpoles, was so called because of his love for plectrum plucking.

Mother, call me Queenie, seated at the far end of the table, replied, 'Pie.'

'And chips, and peas, and vinegar and salt?' voices enquired.

'Yes.'

And with that Mandy was ordered to bring in a magnificent offering, covered in brown pastry, verily groaning on its dish, and, in quick succession, the other essentials of a family dinner.

Father flourished a sharpened knife and plunged it into the entrails of the pie, peeling back pastry to reveal thick brown gravy and a stunning odour, and as they all ducked for cover, four and twenty blackbirds took flight, so Mandy later recalled, spattering gravy, crumbs and meat over the family, furnishings and the recently decorated dining room walls. Two crashed, the cat got one and the rest escaped. Those walls will need repapering, Father thought, counting the change in his pocket.

'Let me put it to you, M'lud, that if you had been torn from the wild and covered in…'

'Yes.'

'And then baked in a pre-heated electric oven at 200°C for forty-five minutes, you would fly around at random, dive-bombing all in sight, given the chance.'

'Point sustained,' Mr Justice Starmer harrumphed.

Wiping his glasses and thinking that a sandwich and beer in the office might have been a better alternative, Ferdinand licked his knife and enquired with kingly sang froid, 'What's for pudding?'

'Dessert,' Queenie corrected.

'Apple pie,' Mandy said, 'made by me.'

And it came about that said pie or tart, as some may call it, appeared amidst the wreckage and was crammed into five hungry mouths without waiting for the custard.

Knock, knock.

'Who's there?'

''tis the Sweeney,' a burly inspector replied. 'I have come to investigate a culinary irregularity,' she continued, 'contravention of the wildlife laws and food hygiene.'

'Phew,' said Ferdinand, 'I thought it might have been the birthday cake affair.'

The inspector cleared a space, moistened the end of her pencil and began to write laboriously in her notebook.

Hungry, she espied a solitary apple, somehow missed by the family. Without a by your leave, she picked it up and bit into the tender flesh, her face contorted, and her soul was winging its way to Scotland Yard.

Mandy smiled and shrugged. She had hoped to get a family member, but this was better than nothing. Memo, more cyanide.

26 January 2022

A Selection of Short, Sometimes Very Short, Stories

JJWUTH

My guest today is Professor Peregrine Prendergast, who, in his own words, is a peripatetic pontificator, prognosticator and perspicacious procrastinator.

'Thank you, my dear Fiona.'

'Today's question concerns updating a well-known nursery rhyme, to make it understandable to the modern child. We at the BBC have chosen "Jack and Jill", which of course has some relevance to the state of the NHS today. Professor what is your take on this?'

'Well, Jack is a bit of a randy lad and his inamorata a post-pubescent, nubile nymph. For reason or reasons unknown, but possibly the consummation of pre-coital urges, these two decided to disguise their intentions by taking a bucket, probably plastic and of ten litres capacity, up a precipitous promontory to procure a supply of potable spring water.'

'That is strange, Professor; surely you don't find water on the top of a hill?'

Indeed, Fiona you are correct, but as in all aspects of life there are exceptions. Physically speaking, water flows down hill, though through a serendipitous association of bedding planes and tectonic activity, the spring might appear at, or towards, the summit.'

'What then, Professor? Poor Jack, gauche and lovelorn, probably consumed with, was it rust you said?'

'No, my dear miss, lust, not rust, he's not your knight in armour, though I suppose one could say amour. However, to return to the story, Jack trips over a protruding pebble and suffers contusions, haematoma, to the right anterior portion of his occipital area, possible sub-cranial injury and maybe even a fractured zygmoidal arch, necessitating immediate medical attention, an MRI scan and the services of a neurologist and maxillary facial surgeon.

'Does the helicopter fly him to A & E?'

'No, no. These two are lovers and the thought of an interminable wait in a crowded hospital is too much for their passion. They stumble down the hillside, spilling the water and consult the homeopathic holistic healer who prescribes vinegar, a mild antiseptic, and paper bandages as these recycle so easily.'

'And does Jack retain his virility?'

'Yes, but he falls into the arms of the healer's assistant, The Sweet Lass of Richmond Hill and forgets poor Jill. She seeks solace in the embrace of the King, counting out his Money, but, having ignored her lessons in home economics, fudges the blackbird pie.'

'Oh no, Professor, it is too much to bear.'

'Don't worry, my dear, I have a happy ending. I see Jack and Jill, transmuted into Derby and Joan. She is sitting by the fire with a black cat at her feet knitting socks for soldiers, while he, puffing on a pipe packed with weed, tries to pick the winner of the Cheltenham Gold Cup on his iPad. But enough, my dear Fiona, of this twisted tale of tortuous trysting; let us two consider a musical meeting with Mussorgsky for a Night on the Bare Mountain; I have the champagne, if you have the appropriate medical paraphernalia.'

13 March 2015

A Tribute

A Tribute

I Remember

You would have been one hundred years old this year, or would it have been last year? My memory is old and cracks are beginning to appear in it, allowing facts to slip away.

I never knew you in person, but I inherited your stamp album, saw some of your exercise books from your time at grammar school, was fascinated by the Frog model aeroplanes in your bedroom, and acquired some of your Hornby railway engines and rolling stock. How I wish I still had those. One day I was given a pile of old, Bakelite, 78rpm gramophone records. One was 'Shepherd of the Hills, I hear you Calling', a pop song of the late 1920s/early 30s. There were some good tunes then!

'Aunty' and 'Unc' were friends of my parents, who lived in a large, undistinguished house, called Wood End, at Tanworth in Arden, to the south of Birmingham. 'Aunty' was plump, rather sad and always wore wire-rimmed spectacles, while 'Unc' was talkative, liked a drink and listened to the racing results on a Saturday. I thought that the horses had ridiculous names. When we visited, 'Unc' would slip me half a crown, then one day it was a ten-shilling note.

We used to go over occasionally to Wood End for tea or simply to talk. The drawing room was spacious with windows on two adjoining sides. The other rooms downstairs were dark and seemed threatening to a young child. The house was set at the end of a long gravel drive lined on one side with tall trees, including a monkey puzzle tree, or for you arboriculturists a Chilean Pine. The long lawn and flower beds sloped down to an equally large, but deserted, vegetable patch. 'Unc' could get an old boy to cut the lawns but no one to 'Dig for Victory.' From one end of the garden to the other there were the remains of a model railway layout.

There was a small, and fortunately, shallow, lily pond in one corner of the garden where I learnt one winter's day that appearances can (and do) deceive. I must have been bored with adult talk, so I slipped out and stepped onto the ice – thin ice. With sopping feet I ran back howling to my mother and was probably comforted with a piece of cake by Hay, the aged maid, while shoes and socks were dried out.

Eighty or eighty-one years ago, Sergeant Pilot Philip John Miles was flying a Spitfire on a routine patrol over Dunoon when the engine failed. In the finest traditions of the RAF he managed to avoid the town but by then he was too low to bail out successfully. His broken body was brought down by train and buried in Christchurch cemetery, Yardley Wood, South East Birmingham.

We received a jubilee clip from the aircraft, which I unfortunately misplaced.

Philip, I salute your memory, young, vital and questing, your life and your sacrifice. May you rest in peace.

14 February 2023

A Tribute

My Inspiration

A host of daffodils, the inscription on a Grecian urn, or a glance at Chapman's Homer?

No, strolling in the grounds of Oxford crematorium just before attending a service for a friend. Not a close friend but someone with whom I had spent many enjoyable hours painting and chatting. A generous man, plagued by ill health but always positive and cheerful.

The roses in the grounds of the crematorium were beautiful though they could have done with some dead-heading and there was the occasional case of black spot – so unlike the few bushes in my garden where I fight a continual battle with that unsightly fungus.

There was a bench in front of one bed of half standard, yellow, roses. And to one side, carefully placed on the concrete plinth to which the bench was secured, a beer bottle, brown, empty, upright, 660 ml I judged, not Newcastle Brown, but a foreign brew, German at the top of the label with Chinese or Japanese characters along the bottom. Is this an example of the post-modern consumerist world? Wary of Covid, and in my best suit, I did not pick up the bottle for further examination or kneel down to look at it more closely.

Did a casual itinerant creep into the grounds of the crematorium to slake her thirst? More likely his thirst, given the nature of the evidence. Why not a wine bottle? A beer bottle is easier to hide under a jacket or pullover.

Perhaps the bottle belonged to a mourner, the contents drunk before the service to steady the nerves, or consumed afterwards to dull the pain of the loss. Maybe someone simply felt thirsty. I checked my watch. Five minutes. Time for me to join the small group at the entrance to the chapel and then say goodbye to my friend.

It was a simple, moving ritual. Now I must concentrate on negotiating that roundabout at Headington, with traffic coming in from all directions.

Back home I change, have lunch and go into the garden to repair the back fence and remove resistant weeds. It's warm work and after an hour, I stop, select a small bottle of lager from the fridge and sit for a while on our garden bench, drinking and listening to the suburban drone of lawn mowers, children's voices, and distant cars.

There is a little more work to do before teatime. I place the empty bottle carefully by the side of the garden bench – mustn't forget to recycle the glass – and finish the weeding.

28 August 2021

A Tribute

An Item Of Memory

It was about eight o'clock on a summer evening. Three of us had eaten at the New B in Parker Street. It was the cheapest curry house in town and gained added publicity from the frequency with which it, or the contents of its food, featured in the local press. We were students, young, invincible and apparently with strong digestions.

It was too late for the cinema and none of us wanted to go drinking. John had an important cross-country race on the morrow and Bill, the tall American ex-navy man, decided to take the night shift in the lab. Maybe his experiment would work properly this time.

As we were about to split up, I saw someone coming towards us. Early twenties, wearing an unbuttoned and rather dirty raincoat, fair hair pushed back from his face, carrying a large battered brown suitcase.

He stopped. 'Where's the YM?' he asked.

My companions were puzzled.

'YMCA hostel.'

'Yeah, that's it.'

'About half a mile down the road.' I pointed. 'Turn right and you can't miss it.'

'I've just hitched up from Wembley,' he volunteered. 'All my gear is in here.' He indicated the suitcase which was on the pavement. 'Thought I'd make a new start.'

He nodded and walked off. No attempt to ask for money, which was unusual.

Why does one chance, inconsequential meeting stay in my memory when so many others fade? What happened to him; did he settle down, have a family, move on? Is he dead now, like my two friends?

I think it was his innocent optimism that impressed me. Unlike us he had no place to stay, probably not much money, no family back-up, but he was prepared to give things a try, have a go.

3 March 2021

A Tribute

Are We There Yet?

'The SatNav never lies.' I tried to put some conviction into my voice.

Alice, with a bottle of wine firmly clamped between her thighs, one hand holding the door handle and the other poised above the dashboard ready to provide instant bracing, scowled. 'Are you sure?'

'It's Boars Hill,' I explained. 'You would expect a few ruts in the lanes and lots of tall trees.'

I heaved the car round a corner and ahead was our destination. I selected the perfect parking space beside the trees. Alice opened her door and smiled icily at me. Mud is not my fault but sometimes silence is better than argument.

The marquee was big, and attached to the side of a two-storey white house by a covered walkway. A woman with recycled blonde hair and a purple sweater was directing newcomers.

'Drinks on the left as you enter and food at the far side,' she said and was on to the next guest.

Alice added our wine, now at blood temperature, to the other bottles on the table. I'll take the car keys.' She held out her hand. Her smile was warmer now.

I wrapped my fist around a tumblerful of red wine and strolled across to the food. I looked over my shoulder and saw that my wife was already chatting to a girl peering at the world from beneath the rim of a shapeless felt hat. How I envied Alice's easy rapport with strangers.

A cauldron of meat was bubbling nearby. Toads and newts? Possibly, knowing our erstwhile host, Joe. Reassurance came from a white face set in a cascade of brown, pre-Raphaelite hair. 'It's beef.' The accent was harsh and disappointing.

'And that,' she added, pointing to a jar, 'is a well-known Icelandic delicacy, preserved shark's meat. It has to be buried for three months before it's ready to eat.'

I gagged. The contents reminded me of the pickled body bits used to greet medical students. That was thirty years ago, and I became an accountant.

'Hello, Alan,' the elegantly dressed Charles greeted me. 'There must be a hundred and fifty here. I wonder if my send-off will attract as many?' He laughed. Before I could reply he added, 'Certainly not wives one and two. First thing they will do when they hear of my demise will be to instruct their respective lawyers. Must circulate, old boy,' and he was off, possibly searching for number three or four.

The whole place was reverberating with voices and music. In a corner a tanned man with a ponytail was exciting a Mongolian singing bowl. Alice was reading the boards detailing Joe's life and times. Out of focus black and white snapshots, high school, university, ethnography, anthropology. Her slim, sexy figure still makes my head spin. I crept up behind her, gently pulled back her hair and found an ear.

'Hi, miss, how about …' The beautiful speech was cut short by the Valkyries riding out from all directions. We were blasted for twenty seconds and then silence. As we recovered from shell shock, the tanned man, now clad in white robes, with a rough wooden crucifix around his neck, introduced himself.

A Tribute

'Hi, folks, I'm Mike, Joe's cousin. Please follow me down to the lake for the committal.'

We filed in twos and threes down a muddy pathway through the trees, picking up guttering candles on the way. Charles was ahead with purple sweater on one arm and white face with long brown hair on the other.

'How does he do it?' I whispered to Alice.

'Charm, money, power,' she replied.

That put me in my place.

It was about a hundred yards to the water. The light was beginning to dim as Mike walked out onto a rickety jetty, dipped a ladle into the wooden bowl he was carrying and scattered the first of the ashes. Three or four more people followed and then he invited each of us to make our own oblation. Alice was one of the first to step forward. My emotions were oscillating between solemnity and nervousness, and I took longer. The fine dust lingered in the air while the heavier material fell into the water, each particle radiating a circular pattern of disturbance on impact, patterns which coalesced and died away, returning the water to tranquillity.

Eventually Mike placed a flickering candle in the bowl and launched it forth upon the lake. I clasped Alice tightly. My candle burnt out. I hardly noticed the soft plop of molten wax on my hand. As the light disappeared forever, behind a small scrub covered island, a bird broke cover and flew off into the fading light.

To cover my feelings, I wondered if it had the right coordinates in its SatNav. Alice must have read my thoughts. She aimed a kick at my ankle and said that she was trying to get a stone out of her shoe.

27 February 2011

A note for the reader
Boars Hill is a large woody area, a few miles SW of Oxford. Explore the paths through the trees, see Jarn Mound and Matthew Arnold's field and, of course, the lake I mentioned.

Finale

A Selection of Short, Sometimes Very Short, Stories

The Last Hill

He loved the stout, brown leather shoes the moment he saw them in the old-fashioned cobblers at the bottom of the main street. He returned every Saturday to gaze at them, make sure they were safe, until he had saved up enough money to buy them.

'Nice shoe, tooled leather, wide welts, you can resole those time and time again', the old man behind the counter said. 'You won't regret buying them.'

'I know,' the younger man replied.

The scrunch when the soles pressed onto gravel or rock, the soft clunk they made when walking on tarmac, was reassuring. It calmed him and made his body and mind feel at one with the massive earth, and somehow helped to counter the perverseness and complexity of life.

The leather had been fed with polish and the soles replaced many times. He had never thrown the shoes away. He couldn't. But neither had he worn them for a decade or more. Now they were restless and demanded his attention. He looked at them and nodded. One more walk. Out of the corner of his eye he thought he caught them smiling at him.

The path up the bracken-covered hillside was made from beaten earth and smoothed rock, worn away by countless feet over many, many years and eroded by the wild water in winter. The track meandered along and upwards in a series of zigzags for nearly a thousand feet to give a grand view of the surrounding plains. It was usually so busy with people, dogs,

Finale

children, lovers, but not now. He knew he was the only person there.

The shoes went steadily on, though every so often his body stopped to gulp in the hot, humid air and to let the thumping heart slow down. Sweat dripped off his brow and spotted the dry ground. He would have liked to have rested rather longer on the old wooden bench, mused on the day and gazed about him, but the shoes forced him, gently but inexorably, onwards. Power from the earth surged up through the leather and pulsed through his body. No peace this evening. Better get on to the summit.

Gradually it became cooler and the insects less troublesome. Every step seemed inevitable and preordained. He couldn't recall exactly why he had come. Maybe it would still his conscience, steady him and take away the insistent throbbing in his temples.

The view from the top was very clear. The dust and haze of the day had been pushed away. The cloud and condensation gone. The surrounding areas were sharply edged and still. He slowly scanned all about him. The small woods and farms and even the hop fields to the west. The flat dwarf-like city to the north with some yellow lights beginning to pick out the streets. The silver scar that he knew was the river. The succession of smaller hills pointing to the tree-topped outlier twenty miles south. People sometimes asked him which was his favourite. He loved them all but if he had to choose it must be the south lands. Hidden down there was the stone monument to some long-forgotten hero of a small, distant and inconsequential war. The tall stone pillar had power and beauty. When you lay at the bottom and looked up at the sky, the stones seemed to topple and topple …

His eyes took it all in and his mind was quiet, peaceful and accepting. He mopped his brow and came out of his reverie. Another day over. Where now?

The shoes knew and urged their owner on. Across the closely cropped and grazed turf so springy that it made walking difficult. Then back onto the stony ridge, past the broken fence posts and rusting, sagging wire to the edge of the deserted quarry gouged out of the hillside to take its precious granite.

How carelessly he and his fellows had used that gift, breaking it into small pieces to build roads or polishing slabs for tombstones and buildings. Water had collected in the bottom of the quarry, fed by several small springs. The area was usually a worldly, noisy playground. Now there was a stillness about it that he could feel and hear. It reminded him of the enchanted mere he had been taken to when he was a small boy.

The air was heavy again, the panorama became misty, and the little stone church beckoned to him. Time slowed down. The body, the soul, the spirit were overcome by a great weariness. He tried to catch his feelings. For once the internal dialogue was stilled.

Go on! Go on! The sound echoed about him and inside him. One shoe stepped over the rocky edge. He tipped forward and the right foot gave the final impetus. His body, uncomprehending, fell and plunged towards the rocks and shallow water several hundred feet below. The water surface, like a mirror in the evening light, exploded, subsided and then nothing remained save a few ripples. His shell was broken, finished. Its visions and cares gone. The shoes remained, wet, ripped, scarred, fulfilled. They had carried out their task and would slowly return to 'The Mother'.

Finale

The hill heaved and sighed, not maliciously, but with an inevitability borne of millions of years of existence. Other bodies had made the gaping quarry and now it had claimed its due. Perhaps it would have to yield another block of rose-red rock to make a fitting memorial. So be it.

8 January 2001, revised 16 January 2006

Printed in Great Britain
by Amazon